Black Crow
White Lie

Candi Sary

To Ann & Howie –
Thanks for
coming to our
reading!

Candi Sary

CASPERIAN
BOOKS

www.casperianbooks.com

ISBN-10: 1-934081-37-X
ISBN-13: 978-1-934081-37-2

For my mom and dad,
Arlene and Marijan Katnich

One

I had a nightmare about red ants eating away at my hands. It woke me up. Trembling, I hid my fisted hands in the small space between my neck and my chin. I stared at the empty pillow on her side of the bed. Peeking up at the small clock, I could barely make out the time. Our cheap motel room was lit only by the dull glow of the neon outside our window.

1:09 a.m. She should have been back by now. I relaxed my chin a little, but still kept my hands close to my neck. I stayed that way for almost twenty minutes, until I heard her key in the door. She stumbled in and rushed to the bathroom. She flushed the toilet over and over to cover up her vomiting. It didn't work this time.

"Carson," she moaned, the ceramic bowl amplifying her moan. "Carson, honey, I need you."

Jumping out of bed, I rushed to her, feeling the cold bathroom tile on my feet. She was bent over the toilet, her hair nearly touching the water. Quickly, my hands gathered up her tangled reddish hair and held it behind her neck. She strained her head to look back at me. Her eyes were wet slits caked with mascara, and her mouth wore a smile too heavy for her to hold.

"You're a good boy, Carson," she whispered just before she threw up one last time. Exhausted, she just collapsed right there on the floor, lying down in an S-shape on the bathroom mat.

"Goodnight, Mom," I whispered. I got down on the floor and, with my back to her, tucked myself into the curve of her body, filling in the upper part of the S she made. I reached behind me and grabbed her limp arm. I wrapped it over me and fell asleep.

The next day, I woke up after eleven in bed. I sort of remembered my mom leading me to the bedroom earlier. I saw that she was already up, drinking her tea in a chair by the window. The drapes were closed. Her hair was still wet from a shower, and now she was wearing a robe, her legs folded up on the chair. Her smile was serene.

"You sleep good, honey?"

"Yeah," I said stretching my arms up above my head, my hands hitting the loose headboard.

"Would you like me to take you to a movie today?" Her voice was soft and sweet. "I'll get you popcorn and soda."

"Okay," I said sitting up and rubbing my eyes.

A McDonald's milkshake was usually my reward for taking care of her after a late night. A movie meant she was really sorry that she drank too much.

"We can take the bus to the big theater that you like," she offered as I got out of bed and grabbed the TV remote. "And we can even sit in the balcony section again if you want."

"That'd be cool," I said, flipping through cartoons.

"But before we go, honey—" Her eyes went soft. "Could I just get you to make my head feel better?" I had this way of making my mom's pains go away. I don't know how I was able to do it, but it showed up when I was really young.

I set the remote back on the dresser and went to my mom's chair. Putting my hands over her head I felt the tiny stars that always came. It felt like thousands of them came pouring out of my hands. I couldn't see them with my eyes; I could only see them with my eyes closed. But I could feel them. They filled my hands with heat, and when I shared them with my mom, they made her feel better.

I don't remember the first time I used the stars, just like I don't remember the first time I used my voice. When I asked my mom how I got them, she said I just knew I had them in me—the same way I knew I had words in me.

Two

Sometimes I wished we were more like other families. I would have liked living in a house instead of motels. I would have liked a mom who stayed home more often and did things like bake cookies and play board games with me. I would have really liked having a dad around, but I got used to our life the way it was. My mom told me it had taken thousands of years for me to find her again. That's a long time to wait for someone special to come back. It was easier appreciating what we had together knowing the whole story.

"It was right here on this same land," my mother explained to me back when I was ten. "We were Indians—Californian Indians. This pale skin," she pinched my arm, "was once native brown. And these legs of yours were once big and strong so that you could run after deer and shoot them with your arrows, and then bring the meat back to me." She leaned back next to me on the olive green couch, wearing a reminiscent smile. The contentment on her face made me wish I could remember our days as Indians. But I only had her stories.

Wrapping her hands around the bottle of wine that sat between her legs, she raised it to her lips and tossed her head back. This motel didn't supply glasses so she drank straight from the bottle. I watched as she poured the last of the wine into her mouth, swallowing steadily until it was emptied. I loved it when my mom told me stories about the ancient days, and I didn't mind the wine because it seemed to help her remember. So I jumped up and ran to the brown paper grocery bag beside the door, shoving aside the white sliced bread and the box of powdered doughnuts to get to the second bottle. I brought it back to the couch for her. The way she smiled at me as I handed it to her was probably how she smiled when I brought her the gift of deer meat in the old days.

"You were my son in that life, too," she went on, her hands caressing the new bottle in her lap. "You were the treasure of our tribe and you were mine." Her lips spread into a smile and her closed eyelids fluttered. "You were destined to be the great medicine man, the great healer who would take away all the pain and disease and suffering of our people. But then—" She opened her eyes and there was terror in them as she looked up over my head. I turned around to see what she was looking at. There was nothing but the old motel room door with the peephole and the silver-chained lock.

I turned back to her wide-eyed. "What, Mom?"

"You were killed," she told me, her voice again firm, her chin held high. "Another tribe attacked us and I was there when the killer shot his arrow into your heart."

I swallowed nervously at the description of my death.

"I lost you." Her eyes began welling and her hands, still wrapped around the bottle, began shaking. "I lost you in that life." Her voice rose as if she was going to cry, but she didn't. "I waited and waited for your soul to come back to me in each life after that, but it never came. I thought I'd never be with you again."

She paused from her story and took to the business of unscrewing the cap on the bottle in her lap. Her gold bracelets clinked together as she twisted her wrist. I loved the sound. The bracelets were a symbol to me that a part of my mom was glamorous. Although we didn't have many advantages in our life, my mom's jewelry made her look like one of those women who did. When she got the bottle open, I could smell the familiar scent of fruit juice and alcohol. It left a sweet sting in my throat.

"Then I gave birth to you in this life," she went on after another drink. "When you were a little boy, you'd make me feel better with your little hands on me and that intent look on your face, like you were wishing my pain away." She smiled. "That's what made me recognize you. I knew you had finally come back to me. For thousands of years we were separated, but fate finally brought you back to me."

She moved closer and grabbed hold of my shoulders, keeping the bottle carefully balanced between her legs. "So it's time that I tell you. It's time that you know. You have finally come back to fulfill your destiny.

Carson," she said looking directly into my eyes, "you are the great healer of our time."

I felt so lightheaded, I thought I was floating.

She took her hands away from my shoulders. Leaning against the couch, she tossed her long, wild hair back and smiled. Her eyes were closed, the bottle still balanced between her legs. "Since you were little, people could tell that there was something special about you. Strangers would stop me on the street and say things like, 'Your boy has a light about him. He's not an ordinary boy, you know. He's special.' But I knew all along what they were seeing."

She grabbed the bottle from between her legs and took a quick drink. "It was cute at first the way you were always caring about making your mom feel better—but then I realized there was more to it. Something miraculous was going on." She nodded her head and smiled. "I thought it was time that I told you the story of your ancient past so you could understand who you really are."

She suddenly took the bottle from her lap and held it up—like she was making a toast. "But enough about the past, Carson. I've also seen your future." She came close and whispered, "They will be drawn to you the way flowers are drawn to the light."

It was the first time my mom had revealed my destiny to me, but I would hear the story over and over as the years went on. Sometimes she would add more details, and other times she would be so drunk she would get to the part about my ancient death and then pass out. I loved hearing the story, even when she was just coherent enough to tell me half of it.

Most people live a whole lifetime without knowing their purpose. Some take years of searching and barely figure it out in their adulthoods. I was the exception, the fortunate child who was clearly handed his life's purpose at the age of ten. I was born to be a healer. And I knew it was true because my mom had told me so.

Three

"You're skinny."

"I know."

"Your clothes are too big for you."

"I know."

"You have to use a lunch card because you don't even have enough money to buy your own lunch."

"I know."

"Your hair is greasy."

My fingers shot up to my head and rummaged through the slick strands of my faded brown bowl cut. I brought my fingers to my nose and took a sniff of the oily residue left on them. It smelled dirty, so I figured it must also look dirty. "I know." I shrugged, looking up at her. She was almost a whole head taller than me.

"You're gross." Rose squeezed her eyes and nose like she was trying to bring them together. "Look, you guys," she addressed the small crowd that had gathered around us on the playground. "Carson smelled the greasy hair stuff on his fingers. He's so gross!"

As her whining voice taunted me, I scoured my fingers through my oily hair again and then thrust them toward her nose. "Now you're gross 'cause you smelled it too."

She might have made the surrounding girls giggle at her teasing, but I made the boys crack up. They didn't even care that I was skinny or greasy if I could actually stand up to Rose Lewis, the bitchiest girl in fourth grade. Rose—I wondered if she was named for the thorns instead of the flower.

"I hate you, Carson Calley," Rose cried. The boys were still laughing and even some of the girls looked like they were trying to hold back smiles. "You're ugly and you're—you're—" It seemed she couldn't find a word repulsive enough to describe me. "You're *sick,*" she finally cried, a little spray of spit following the last word.

I didn't like what she was saying about me, but I knew from experience that there was nothing I could do to get someone like her to stop. All I could do was maintain my cool. So I said again those two defiantly agreeable words my mom had taught me to use against bullies back in second grade. "I know."

That's when she grabbed my arms, digging her fingernails into my skin, and tried to throw me toward the crowd. I lost my balance and hit the blacktop hard, landing awkwardly on my right hip and elbow. The pain was almost as bad as all the laughter that was now directed at me. I had managed to stay cool up to that point, but it was as if the fall had sent a jolt through me, unleashing a load of anger I was holding inside.

I picked myself up and, like a charging bull, I rushed toward her with my head down. My eyes clung to her white shoes with the purple laces as I punched my head into her stomach and my hands pushed her shoulders. All the tangled feelings I had inside of me exploded in that brief moment when I slammed into her. She fell back onto the ground, the wind knocked out of her. She was down, gasping for breath and then crying. I stood there stunned at what I had done.

I had never hurt anyone before. I was supposed to be a healer. It didn't make sense for me to *give* pain. Sometimes I took my anger out on things when I was mad, but just things—like the stuff in our motel room. I had never hurt a person, and certainly never thought I had it in me to hit a girl. I didn't know what do. I watched as the other girls helped Rose up. I wanted to say I was sorry, but I couldn't. I just stood there, feeling like a bully when I knew I wasn't.

Four

Most of the kids from school lived in the neighborhoods on the outskirts of the city, but I lived in a variety of motels right near the heart of Hollywood. Sometimes when I became restless in the cramped little room of a motel, or just craved more sunlight, my mom would say, "Why don't you go play out front for a while?" It sounded so ordinary to *go play out front.* Walking out of the room, through the lobby (a few of the places we stayed at had lobbies), I'd create a picture in my mind of a traditional front yard and pretend that was where I was headed. I'd walk with a little bounce in my step and a swing to my arms—like one of those kids who had their own lawn—and I'd smile and wave at the guy at the front desk pretending he was just a neighbor. Those were the moments when I felt like every other ordinary kid.

Once out front, though, I was immersed in the untraditional life of Carson Calley. I'd see the outrageous, the flamboyant, and the funky people of Hollywood walking down the streets as if on their way to something big. Everything is extra big in Hollywood—hopes, dreams, successes, failure. Even mediocrity has a way of looking big in Hollywood.

I would walk or skateboard the neighborhood and visit some of my favorite spots. House of Freaks, a tattoo shop, was usually my first stop. I loved to check out all the designs in the window. A guy named Faris owned House of Freaks. The first time I saw him, it was summertime and he was standing outside the door smoking a cigarette. His head was shaved, and instead of hair, he had overlapping, colorful tattoos on his scalp that crawled down his neck and his chest, and then onto his arms and legs. Everything except his face was tattooed. He looked like a live page from a comic book. He was scary and cool at the same time. When I got real close to him, I noticed an amazingly detailed eagle on his left arm. Trapped in the eagle's massive talons was a naked woman. I couldn't help but stare.

"Wanna touch her titties?"

Startled by his deep voice, my eyes shot up to meet his. Staring back at me was a severe face with bloodshot eyes, worn-out skin, and pale, cracked lips that loosely held his cigarette.

"I, um—okay," I said, not because I wanted to touch them, but I didn't know what else to say.

His laugh was even deeper than his talking voice, but it wasn't as intimidating. "Then come on over and touch 'em," he said, holding his arm out to me.

I took five timid steps and I was standing right beside the comic-book man. I raised my forefinger and middle finger—like I was making a peace sign—and quickly tapped the tattoo.

"Real ones feel a lot better than these. You've got a little time for that." I swallowed hard and then nodded my head. "But you'll remember me the first time you touch the real ones. You'll say, 'That Faris was right. These feel good.'" He tossed his head back and laughed again.

This guy was weird, I thought, but I managed a smile.

"What's your name, kid?" he asked, flinging the last of his cigarette onto the sidewalk.

"Carson."

"How old are you?"

"Twelve." His eyes widened—probably because I was still pretty small for twelve.

"Where you live?"

"Me and my mom are staying at the Starlight."

"Ah," he said with a nod as if my answer was code for some deeper message. "I gotcha."

"I gotta go," I said abruptly. I wanted to get away. He was kind of nice but he made me uncomfortable.

"I'll see you later, Carson."

I avoided House of Freaks after that and found other streets of Hollywood to explore. But Faris was always on my mind. Every time I saw someone with a tattoo, I thought of him. A few months later, I found myself over that way again. Faris was outside and remembered me. He waved me over and we talked for while. He wasn't as scary to me as he had been. Maybe it was because I'd been thinking about him, but he seemed friendlier than before. So I started stopping by more often. The more I talked to him and the closer I looked at his face, the less intimidating he became. There was something soothing about all the wrinkles that dug deep into his skin. I think it was because they mostly showed up when he smiled.

Faris was easy to talk to. He was okay with anything I told him. Sometimes I had to be careful talking to adults about my life. Not everyone thought my stories were alright for a kid to be telling, but Faris seemed to understand me. It started with small stories, just trivial things I wanted to talk about. Faris always listened. And nothing bothered him. So I kept going to him whenever I couldn't get something off my mind.

"She came home the other night," I told him one day. Faris was sitting in the shop paying bills. "And she went right to bed in her clothes and shoes and everything. She didn't go to the bathroom before falling asleep, and I guess because she drank a lot when she was out, she wet the bed." I looked over to see his reaction. He just nodded without saying anything. "That never happened before," I let him know. "Just this one time. She told me it was an accident and she was really embarrassed by it 'cause, you know, kids do that sometimes, but not moms." Faris still didn't say anything. He just kept his eyes on the bills in front of him as he wrote. "But I guess even if you're a mom and you drink too much before you fall asleep, an accident like that could happen. I bet it could happen probably to anyone."

That was when he finally said something. "I bet it could," he agreed.

"Yeah," I said, feeling a little lighter. If Faris thought it could happen to anyone, then it really could. I felt like I could finally let the incident go.

I took off my sweatshirt and got comfortable on the couch there in the shop while Faris wrote out checks, stuck them in envelopes, and sealed them. I watched what he was doing, but paid more attention to the hands and arms that were doing it all.

"Did it hurt getting all those tattoos?" I asked him.

"Sure it hurt some," he said rubbing his hand over his bald, inked head. "But you get used to it."

"One day I want to get one," I told him.

"Yeah?" He didn't look up, just kept writing.

"I never thought so before, but seeing some of yours, I think it'd be cool to have one. Remember the black widow you did for that guy last week? I really liked that one."

"Yeah, that one turned out okay," he said, looking over at me and nodding. "But you just wait until you find something that means a lot to you before you get one. These are forever."

I tried thinking of something that meant a lot to me, but couldn't come up with anything. I just knew that when I did think of it, I wanted Faris to do it for me.

Five

A peculiar face can really grow on you once it becomes familiar. I know this to be true because it happened with Faris, and then it happened again months later when I met Casper.

Casper worked at a head shop about eight blocks down from House of Freaks, on Sunset Boulevard. I met him one day when my mom sent me there on an errand. He was a tall, lanky albino in his early twenties, with lavender eyes and white dreadlocks. I kept staring at him when we first met because I'd never seen anyone like him. Casper was sweet-looking, angelic even. His pale skin sort of glowed. He wore a black poncho, making his skin look extra pasty, and had a Rastafarian beanie on his head.

"Hello," he greeted me when I walked in. "Can I help you find something?" His voice was friendly and formal, like a bank teller or one of the guys at the welfare office. Somehow, it didn't match his looks.

"I gotta buy a smudge stick," I told him, looking down at the glass case filled with pipes and incense and herbs. Reggae music drifted out from the speakers above.

"Is there a specific smudge stick you're looking for?"

"It's for my mom," I told him. "She needs sage and sweet grass."

"Sage and sweet grass," he repeated as he reached into the glass case and rummaged through the bundled herbs. "Is your mom a priestess?"

"She's a psychic," I told him. "She always burns a smudge stick before a session to clear away negative energy." He didn't respond. His head was still hidden behind all the clutter in the case. "She sees mostly aspiring actors and actresses. My mom says they're the hungriest for knowing their future. She'll never run out of customers in Hollywood. That's why we live here."

Not a word from him. I figured that wasn't interesting enough to this guy, so I thought of something else that might peak his interest. "Her name used to be Maggie Calley, but she legally changed it—to Juliette Bravo." There was still no response. I stood on my toes and leaned over the counter to see if he was okay back there. Suddenly he popped up holding a smudge stick. I fell back on my heels.

"Here we go," he said, setting it on the counter. "So." He gave me his full attention. "Is she a priestess?"

I narrowed my eyes. "I said she was a psychic."

He gave off a puff of laughter. "Sorry, I couldn't hear you while I was down there. My hearing is bad."

"Why's your hearing bad?"

"Long story." He smiled, taking my smudge stick to the cash register. "Maybe next time you come in I'll tell you about it."

"Okay," I said and paid for the stick.

He stared at me for a while. "Tell your mom if she has a flyer or something, I'll put it up."

"Thanks. I will."

"See you later."

All the way home that afternoon, I tried coming up with theories as to how a guy like Casper could have ended up in a head shop. His professional manner didn't quite mesh with the vibe there. Even in a place like Hollywood, it struck me as odd. But he was the kind of guy who would pretty much seem out of place anywhere he worked. He was born not to fit in. Sort of like me. He probably had a good story to tell.

I liked stories. I liked the way they had the power to make sense of life. You could go through a chaotic experience and come out of it feeling confused, but once you tell it to someone as a story, somehow it starts making sense. And I liked watching people cross over to that place that made sense as they retold their tales. I felt like I had company in that safe place away from chaos.

Six

On top of her head was a cascade of uncombed hair sprouting from a rubber band. Her hair verged on red, but was softer—more like cinnamon. My mom leaned toward the table and the long cinnamon strands became a curtain over her face as well as her tea cup. Wearing only a white T-shirt and panties, she stretched out her bare legs toward my chair. Her toenails were painted blue and her long, bony legs were pale and smooth, like porcelain. She tapped her fingernail on the table—the agitation making her bracelets clink. She stayed hidden behind her hair. It had been a late night. I could tell she hadn't gotten much sleep.

"'There is no remedy for love but to love more.' Henry David Thoreau."

On mornings when she didn't have coffee, my mom drank jasmine green tea. Each tea bag had a message on the tag dangling from the string. She always read them to me.

I waited. I couldn't tell if she was going to dispute this one or agree so I didn't give an opinion.

"You can only cure the pains of love by loving more." She tossed her hair behind her and was looking up toward the ceiling. The tiny diamond strung on her gold necklace rested against her pale chest. Her doll-like brown eyes looked as tired as they always did, and her full lips were stuck in their usual wistful smile.

"When love hurts, you don't push it away and banish it from your life. No, you dive deeper and deeper, and once you get deep enough, you find a place where love doesn't hurt anymore." She was talking more to herself than to me.

"How can love hurt?" I asked, pouring milk into the miniature cereal box that acted as a bowl.

My mom's glassy eyes dropped from their perch on the ceiling down to me. She had a worn-out kind of beauty—like a thirsty flower. "It hurts when the one you love is unable," she quickly changed her wording, "no, *unwilling*, to give you what you need." It all sounded vague and foreign to me, but I had a feeling I knew what that meant to her.

"You mean Jackson?" Jackson was my mom's boyfriend. They'd been together a long time but I barely knew him. He liked my mom. He just didn't like that she had a kid.

My mom gave me one of those smiles that told me she adored me. Her fingers caressed the small diamond around her neck. She held onto it as she got up from her chair and went into the tiny kitchenette with the green and yellow flowery wallpaper. "Jackson is not giving me what I need. And I thought that meant that I should shut him out. But the gods have spoken."

She released the diamond and reached for the cabinet. She grabbed a couple of Twin Dragon Almond Cookies from their pink box and brought them back to the table on a paper napkin. "They're telling me that I just need to love him more."

"You think the gods could send a message like that on a tea bag?"

"Oh, the gods are sneaky." Her smile lifted on only one side. "They communicate with us in countless ways, but we don't always notice the signs. If you pay close attention to everything, and don't discount anything, then you have a better shot at hearing what they're trying to tell you."

I looked down at my cereal box. Lucky Charms. I wondered if the gods were trying to tell me that I was going to have a lucky day. I ran my finger over the yellow word on the box.

"So, sweetheart, I think this means I need to spend some more time with Jackson tonight," she told me, breaking a cookie in half. I knew exactly what that meant. She would be out late again and I would be in the motel alone. So much for my lucky day.

"But couldn't he just come here?" I asked.

"You know he doesn't like to do that."

"But what do you guys do all night that you have to come home so late?"

"We go out dancing and, I don't know, we hang out with friends." She took out the rubber band and ran her fingers through her hair. With a deep breath, she explained, "I have to play two very different roles, Carson, to please the two men in my life. When I'm with you, I'm a mom. When I'm with Jackson, I'm a woman."

"They're not the same thing?"

She considered my question for a moment, gingerly tugging the string as the tea bag bobbed in the hot water. "You would think," she spoke softly, her eyes closed.

"Please don't go tonight, Mom. Couldn't we just—"

"I am stuck in the middle between two people I love very much. I can't imagine my life without you or Jackson." Her hands began trembling. She could barely hold the tea cup and a little spilled on the table. She grabbed her napkin and let the cookies drop on the table. Bunching up the napkin, she patted the spilled tea with an agitation that made more of a mess. Her bracelets gave off their familiar noise.

"I love you, Carson." She began to cry. "I love you with all my heart. But I can't survive on mother love alone. I need a man's love, too." Sniffling and clearing her throat, she continued patting the moist napkin on the wet table. "I am working so hard to get Jackson to see that we could be together—me, you, and him—and make a family. He's just afraid. He has to come to that decision on his own. And the more he loves and needs me, the closer he gets to coming home with *us*. Do you understand that at all?"

I nodded. It felt like less of a lie if I didn't use my voice.

Sitting there with my mom, I felt the anger start inside me. I wanted it to go away because it made me want to hit something, anything. The feeling was bigger than me—too big for me to control sometimes. The urge made me tighten my fists under the table.

"Good," she whispered with a grateful smile. "You're a good boy."

"I just wish my dad didn't have to die when I was a baby," I told her keeping my fists tight. "We could have all been together—all the time." My mom didn't say anything. She just rested her head in her hands on the table and quietly cried.

She left around seven that night.

Some nights when she was gone, I watched TV or read through the books she brought home. Sometimes I made up games or daydreamed or even played with imaginary characters. I did my best to be the good boy my mom thought I was. But every once in a while I was too angry about her leaving me to be with Jackson. Those were the nights I gave in to a feeling that was bigger than me.

One night I vandalized two bikes that were left in the bike rack behind the motel, kicking in the spokes and bending the rims. I once messed up the motel landscaping, ripping out flowers from the plastic planters along the back parking lot, and throwing the dirt everywhere. When I was hurt and angry, I found myself doing things that I wouldn't normally have done. There was a fire growing within me, and sometimes my calm nature couldn't compete with the flames.

That night after my mom left, I went downstairs and was immediately drawn to the small room where the ice machine was. It was isolated, dark, and a little scary—the perfect place to do what I had to do. I slammed my fist into the walls over and over again. I watched as my knuckles began to bleed, but I felt nothing shift, no relief. So, gripping my bloodied knuckles, I looked around for a better target.

I noticed a door at the back of the room. It was old and didn't hang evenly on the door frame. I rushed to it, shoving my whole body into it, and forced it open. Inside was a storage room with big boxes of toilet paper on the floor. Keyed up by what I'd discovered, I started kicking at the boxes like a ninja. I broke through them and kept kicking until the rolls were in tatters.

Plowing through the white mess, I went to the back of the room. There were more boxes on shelves. I ripped a couple open and found candy and chips that must have been stock for the vending machine. I tore open more boxes and threw the snacks to the ground. I grabbed some M&Ms and Corn Nuts and stuffed them in my pockets before I started ninja-kicking the rest of the boxes off the shelves, and then stomping on the fallen bags. I might have done more damage if I hadn't heard a car door shut. And then keys jingling from the parking lot just off the small room. My heart pounded. The ninja disappeared and I was once again just a kid—a kid who could get into a lot of trouble.

I ran across the walkway and was back up the stairs by the time the jingling keys had made it to the building. Quickly, I slipped back into my room. Safe inside, I gasped for air. I collapsed against the locked door and slid to the ground. As my pulse slowed along with my breathing, I managed to come back to myself.

Sitting there with my back against the door, I dug into my pocket and grabbed the M&Ms. I ripped open the bag and poured the chocolates in my hand. I didn't want to think about what I'd just done, so I busied my mind with separating all the colors and setting them on the carpet in bunches.

I ate all the green ones first. Then I tossed the others, one at a time, in the air and tried to catch them with my mouth. I missed a lot, so after a while, I quit and just ate them all. It was when I heard a police siren downstairs that I got up from my spot against the door and went to the bathroom to clean up the blood on my hand. I was careful not to use any towels. I used toilet paper so I could flush the evidence down the toilet. Looking at my raw knuckles, I figured I could tell my mom that I was trying to catch myself from falling off my skateboard and I landed wrong.

To my relief, my mom and I ended up moving to another motel the next week. My mom had heard there was some kind of break-in the night she was out and didn't feel comfortable leaving me alone while a criminal was lurking about. I wasn't comfortable being left alone either, since the criminal was closer than she realized.

Seven

It was only the second night in our new motel room and my mom had left me alone, disappearing while I was at school without leaving a note. Not that she'd ever left one before. I hadn't adjusted to the place yet and didn't feel comfortable by myself. At least the rage didn't come over me that night—just loneliness. I wanted company. I decided to walk to the head shop and see if I could catch Casper before they closed. I still hadn't gone back to hear his story.

I stopped at a Mexican food place on the way since it was Taco Tuesday and all tacos were only a dollar. My mom had left a five on the dresser, so I bought five and took them with me to the head shop.

I got there just after eight, and the CLOSED sign was up. But I could see a light on. I placed my forehead against the window and looked inside. I saw his white dreads leaning over the cash register. "Hello," I called out as I knocked on the glass. I hadn't learned his name yet, so I just kept calling out, "Hello." But he didn't look up. So I knocked harder, and called out louder, realizing his hearing was bad. When I finally got his attention, he walked toward the front squinting his eyes. He continued squinting even when he was right at the window looking at me.

It took him a few seconds of staring, but then he smiled and nodded as he unlocked the door for me. "Well, hello again," he said letting me in.

"Hi." I stepped into the warm place that smelled like incense.

"What brings you here this late? Does your mom need another smudge stick?"

"No, I was just," I shrugged, "just in the area and thought I'd stop by."

"Oh," he said, tipping his head toward his shoulder and sort of studying me.

"Wondered if you had some time to tell me that story. About how you messed up your ear."

"You came back," he looked down at his watch, "to hear my story?"

"Yeah," I shrugged again.

"Well, I am almost done closing up the shop," he said. "I was going to head up to my apartment and eat something. Maybe you can come by tomorrow when we're open."

I held up the bag in my hand. "I got five tacos from Taco Tuesday and I don't have to eat all five. You can have a couple."

"Oh, I don't want to take your dinner," he said.

"No, really, I just want three. You can have two of them," I said pulling out two tacos wrapped in foil. I handed them to him.

He was hesitant at first, but then took them. The way he smiled at me, I had the feeling he knew I was just looking for some company. "This is very nice of you," he said.

We ate standing up, using the counter as our table, and that was when I finally asked his name and told him mine. Having dinner together like that, it felt like we were already friends.

It didn't take too long to finish our tacos. When we were done, he led me to a big green beanbag behind the counter. Leaning up against the glass case, facing me, he began his story. As I stared his way, it almost looked like he had a light bulb inside of him lighting up his skin.

"Okay," Casper folded his arms, catching two of his white dreads in the fold. He jerked his head back to release them, and then went on. "It was just a few years ago. I was nineteen years old. A friend of mine shared a special mushroom with me—it's not the kind you find at the grocery store. It's a kind you eat to have new experiences."

I sunk deeper into the beanbag as he spoke. I was relaxed, though my left hand instinctively gripped the bandaged knuckles on my right hand. I wanted to keep them hidden so Casper wouldn't ask about them.

"What happens is your brain sees and experiences things that aren't really there," he said.

"You hallucinate?" I asked.

"Yes. Mushrooms are a kind of drug that makes you hallucinate."

"So the mushrooms messed up your hearing?"

"Well, indirectly you might say. Allow me to finish the entire story." He spoke like a teacher—just didn't look like one. "Having eaten a mushroom, I had this sensation that the house was melting around me, as if closing in on me. I had to run outside to escape getting smothered."

My eyebrows shot up. "Were you scared?"

"Actually, I thought it was kind of funny."

"Why?"

"It wasn't scary at the time since the walls were melting in friendly rainbow colors—yellows, oranges, purples, reds, greens."

Melting walls, no matter what color, sounded like a nightmare to me, but I nodded so that he'd go on.

"So when I got outside, there was a huge tree and I could hear it breathing. Its breath was so calm, I wanted to sit with it. So I went up to its trunk and when I looked closer, I saw it had the shape of a long robe." He widened his eyes and the corners of his mouth slowly lifted in an ominous smile. "It was the Virgin Mary."

"On the tree?"

He nodded his head rapidly. "I worried that the calm breathing meant that she was sleeping, and I didn't want to disturb her. So I tiptoed over to a bush nearby that seemed to be taking heavier breaths. As it breathed, its branches swayed like it was dancing. And then it asked me if I would dance with it. It seemed like a friendly bush so I went along."

I listened, unable to decide which was more peculiar, the story or the storyteller.

"I wrapped my arms around the bush and swayed along with it. It kept whispering for me to get closer and closer and then it told me to rest my head on its shoulder. As soon as I tilted my head to rest on its shoulder I saw this amazing blast of color that wouldn't go away even when I closed my eyes. There was a lot of red pulsing toward me, and when I looked down it had spread onto my clothes. I sort of passed out."

"Was your friend still with you?"

"I don't know what happened to him. When I woke up, I was alone. And that's when I felt a sharp pain in my ear. Looking down, I saw that my shirt was covered with blood. I realized that when I'd leaned my head into the bush, a branch made its way into my ear. That's how I injured my ear drum. And I've been deaf in that ear ever since."

I cringed and instinctively brought my hand up to my own ear.

"Yes." He nodded at my reaction. "I learned the hard way. When you give yourself over to substances that take control of you, you take some serious risks. I lost my hearing—that was my lesson."

He continued talking to me, but I could tell it was going to remain one of those one-way conversations where he didn't want me saying anything to interrupt him. So I sat on the beanbag listening to him tell stories as I focused on the way his white eyelashes and white nose hair looked almost transparent from my view below him.

I liked to listen to people. When people found that out about me, they would talk and talk, like Casper ended up doing that night. I would hold their words in my mind as if saving the words in case they needed them later. That's what I often did for my mom. If she came home late at night with wild stories about where she'd been, I'd have to remember the details so that I could tell her the next morning since the alcohol often wiped the memories away.

When Casper finally opened up the conversation to me, I had only one response to give. "I can heal you," I told him.

"How?" he turned his head a little to look at me from the corner of his eye.

I wasn't sure if the tiny stars could heal his ear the way it healed my mom's headaches and stuff, but I knew I needed to try my gift on other people to see what I was capable of. Here was my opportunity. I stood up from the beanbag and approached him. I reached my hands out toward him, but then squeezed them into fists. My heart started beating faster and I felt this terrible moment of doubt. What if it didn't work after I told him I could do it? I pulled my hands back.

"Are you okay?" he asked.

"Yeah," I said, trying to think up an excuse for pulling away. "I just need to start with a turquoise stone. Do you have one?" My mom once told me that I wore a lot of turquoise back in my Native American lifetime because the stone had healing powers. I figured it might help me in this lifetime as well.

"Turquoise?" He said it suspiciously.

"Turquoise." I tried to remain firm.

Casper walked away, and rummaged through the woven basket on a shelf behind him. I took some deep breaths and spread out my fingers, trying to bring up the stars. My hands got a little warmer. I could feel them coming. I was hopeful.

When Casper brought the stone back, I held it in my hand and he just stared at me. That was when I got nervous again. My hands went cold. I just didn't know if my healing power could connect with someone other than my mom. "What time is it?" I asked.

He looked down at his watch. "It's almost nine already."

"Oh, shoot, I was supposed to be back home by nine," I lied, trying to save myself from failing. "I'm not gonna have time to do it right now. But I'll come back."

"Okay." he dropped his head and I could see him smiling. "No problem."

"When I come back next time, I'll heal your ear," I promised.

He looked up at me, still smiling and just said, "Thank you for the tacos, Carson. That was really nice of you to share."

✳ ✳ ✳

Confidence is the most mysterious power of all. My mom taught me that when I asked her if doubt ever effected her ability to predict someone's future.

"Those days when I'm feeling off and out of focus, and I don't know what the hell I'm talking about," she told me, "I just dish 'em up whatever pops into my head, like I'm a hundred percent sure of myself. Not ninety-nine, but a full hundred percent. And by god, they always believe me."

We were getting ourselves settled into the Vine Motel—our latest new home. We'd only stayed in the last motel six nights. I didn't know what had happened, but my mom said we had to move again.

"Isn't that lying?" I asked.

"Of course not," she said. "It's not a lie. Think of it as a creative way to get to the truth."

I unpacked while we talked. Opening a dresser drawer, I found one of those green Bibles they had in all the motels. I shoved it far back into the drawer so I could put my T-shirts and jeans inside. My mom was putting our pillows on the bed and stuffing the motel pillows in the closet.

"But it's not the truth," I said.

"Oh, honey, I'm not explaining myself well, am I? I wouldn't *lie*," she explained with more of a motherly tone, unlike the frivolous tone she'd started with. "Even when I'm out of focus and don't think I know what the hell I'm talking about, the gods still plant things in my head. Sometimes I don't have control over what they put in here," she said wrapping her hands over the top of her head. "So no matter what I end up telling my clients, even if I don't understand it, I say it without any trace of doubt because it must be true. Never question the gods, honey."

"So are you right every time you tell someone their future?" I asked, climbing on the bed next to her. I could smell her shampoo—fruity, like mangoes or peaches.

"It's all about that hundred percent." Her voice was hushed, like she was telling a secret. "More important than my power to predict is my power to get them to *believe.*"

My head sank into the soft pillow as I turned toward her. "Do the gods really send you messages?"

She looked into my eyes for a long few seconds before responding. "Absolutely," she said without a fraction of doubt. I nodded my head, knowing it was true.

It was clear what I'd been missing that night at the head shop with Casper. I already had the power, I just needed the confidence to use it—not seventy, eighty, or even ninety percent. I needed to bring one hundred percent.

Eight

I was on a wooden crate that leaned against the brick wall of the tattoo shop. Faris sat on a stool beside me. When he had no customers, he told me he liked to sit outside in the fresh air and smoke. There was always something interesting to watch in the neighborhood. Everyday Hollywood wasn't the glamorous movie star capital like its reputation on TV. You didn't see many celebrities in our part of town. Sitting out in front of the tattoo shop, we were mostly entertained by peculiar random people walking by.

Another source of entertainment came from across the street. There was a radio station right across from House of Freaks that often had protesters outside. Faris explained that the station had programs with strong opinions promoting one political party, and so people from the opposite party came to protest the things they said. Protestors marched around in circles with big posters, shouting things, which sometimes made the station people come outside and shout back. It would turn into a drama that was better than the stuff on TV, and so TV news cameras came to capture the good fighting without even having to pay actors. We practically had front-row seats there at Faris' place. But there were no protestors that day, so we had to settle on watching the random people on the sidewalks.

"Your dad live around here?" Faris asked before taking a long drag of what was left of his cigarette.

"I don't have a dad anymore. He died."

"Sorry to hear."

"You know my dad was a hero," I said with a rapid nod.

"A hero, huh?"

"Yeah, and he was even buried at the Cemetery of Heroes—that one in Washington DC where lots of war heroes are buried?" Faris nodded. "But he has like this whole section of the cemetery to himself—'cause he was pretty important."

"Must be to have a whole section to himself."

"My mom says we'll save up money one day and go bring flowers to his grave."

"What branch of the military was he in?"

"He was in like the special forces that no one knew about. In fact, he wasn't even allowed to tell my mom everything. But he told her some."

"So tell me what you know." Faris dropped the tiny nub that was still lit on the end. It landed near his foot and he lightly tapped it with his worn flip-flop. I noticed a snake wrapped around his ankle, its eyes looking up at a woman in a bikini playing a flute. I squinted and leaned forward, noticing her long red fingernails. Faris pulled his foot back toward his stool, and I sat straight up again. He leaned back on the wall and folded his colorful arms.

"Well," I went on, "he told my mom how he flew in a one-man plane that couldn't be detected by radar, and it could land just about anywhere. So he was able to sneak into other countries and take care of secret business."

"Hm, one-man plane. Secret business. Sounds dangerous."

"Yeah. I have one of his medals that my mom saved for me. He was really a hero. He would go into countries with corrupt governments and he'd take out the worst, evil men. He was so good, even the president knew him personally. I mean if he was alive back in the 1940s, he could've even destroyed Hitler and we'd never even have had that whole Holocaust." I heard in school about what Hitler did and I knew my dad wouldn't have let him get away with it.

"Sounds like quite a guy," Faris said, languorously reaching down to scratch his leg, right above the snake.

"And he didn't even have to use a gun," I told him, my voice getting louder as I grew more excited the deeper I got into the story. "He could slaughter someone with his bare hands."

"Sounds like he had some serious hands," he said, holding up his own hands, fingers spread wide. He had an intricate pattern of jagged lines across his fingers, with small designs that looked like Chinese writing.

At this point I was sitting at the edge of the wooden crate, barely supported by it. "One time he even showed my mom how quick and powerful he was. They were sitting outside in the backyard. When my dad was alive, they had a big house in Beverly Hills with a huge backyard and a pool." I waited for a response to this impressive bit of information.

"Sounds like your dad must've been pretty big time."

"Yeah, my mom said he was." I lost my balance a little and had to scoot back on the crate. "So he threw some bread crumbs out on the lawn and sat real still next to them. Then some black crows came down to eat the bread, and since my dad was sitting so still, they weren't afraid of him. But just as one landed right next to him, he grabbed it," I said, shooting out my arm in front of me. "With a single motion, he broke its neck." My wrist twisted so fast, it almost snapped. I could feel my heartbeat up in my throat, and I almost felt winded. "He caught the black crow with his bare hands and killed it in like a second."

Faris just sat back staring out into the street for a while, not actually looking at the cars, but sort of looking through them. He finally leaned toward me and looked right into my eyes. "That's some story. Sounds like you come from damn good blood."

"Yeah," I agreed, looking right back into his eyes.

He began shaking his head and he pursed his dried, cracked lips. "I heard enough of your stories these past few months to know a little something about your life. I know that your mom needs a little more help from the bottle than most."

The rhythm of my blood suddenly stuttered and I felt like I'd dropped ten feet from my euphoric high. What did my mom's drinking have to do with what we were talking about? I sat motionless, waiting to hear the connection.

"Maybe drinking's the only way to ease her pain over losing a great man like your dad. I don't know." He leaned back against the brick wall. "Whatever her reason, I don't want you falling into the same disease she's got. You just always remember that half of you was made from the man who could catch and kill a black crow with his bare hands. You can't dishonor a man like that by being a weak son who wastes away his life. I expect great things from you when you grow up, you hear me?"

"Disease?" I voiced the only word that stuck with me.

"Yeah." His tone was apologetic. "There's this disease you can get in your head, and you start thinking the only cure is alcohol. But in fact al-

cohol is not a cure—it's what feeds the disease. Trust me. I been there."
He tried to smile and deep lines formed all over his face.

"But my mom doesn't have that," I asserted. "She's fine."

He smiled softer and looked at me for a few seconds. "Ah, what the hell
do I know." He laughed. "You're right. I don't know your mom except from
a few stories. Just 'cause I had the disease when I drank doesn't mean
everyone who drinks has got it, right?" He dug into his pocket and pulled
out a fresh cigarette. "Now this here is a disease," he said holding the
small white stick up to his lighter. He started to laugh. His laugh transitioned into a hacking cough and he had to go inside the shop to get a glass
of water. I stayed there on the crate, thinking about what he'd said, still
trying to figure out why he brought up my mom when I'd just told him the
best story I knew about my dad.

Nine

My mom had a headache again. Over the years, her pains gave me opportunities to practice my healing powers. But sometimes she didn't want me to use the stars on her. Sometimes she just asked for a simple massage, saying that plain old human touch had its own kind of magic.

I rubbed her back and neck with eucalyptus oil. She lay on her stomach on the couch while I knelt on the floor beside her. When I was little I used to sit straddled on her hips, but I could tell I was getting taller. At twelve, my legs didn't tuck so easily in the couch anymore.

"Is it true that some people can get a disease from drinking alcohol?" I asked.

She didn't answer.

"I heard that you could," I said making small circles at the base of her neck with my thumbs. A little eucalyptus oil had seeped into the scabs on my knuckles. These newest scabs were from the night I almost got caught punching in the newspaper dispenser in front of the bus stop by the motel. A guy across the street saw me and yelled out, "Hey!" but couldn't keep up with me as I ran and ran. The scabs had almost healed, but I felt a slight sting where the skin hadn't completely closed up.

"How do you know when you have that disease?" I asked her.

"I don't know, since I don't have it." Her words were drowsy and muffled as she spoke into the couch.

"So what happens to people who do have the disease?"

"They get addicted to it and can't stop drinking."

"Can you stop if you wanted to?"

"Never tried. I don't want to."

"Even when it makes you feel sick?"

She strained her neck and lifted her head to look at me. Her knotted hair covered half of her face. "What the hell is this?" She was tired but still sounded firm. "What's with all the questions?"

"I was just asking."

She dropped her head again and breathed in. "I only drink at night," her tone eased. "You don't see me drinking during the day, or when I'm with a client. When you have the disease you drink all the time. I *choose* when I drink."

"Oh." I began using the edge of my palm, between my thumb and wrist, to massage her lower back muscles.

"And I drink to relax," she added. "I use a lot of energy in my job. My mind takes a beating some days. Sometimes the gods give me too much." She was quiet. I thought our conversation had ended.

"Jackson wouldn't let me get the disease," she said unexpectedly. Her voice was soft. I leaned in closer to her so I could hear. "He always stops me if I've had too much. He's protective of me that way." I knew Jackson was protective of my mom the way he always walked her to the door to make sure she got home okay. That was the only time I ever got glimpses of him. From the doorway, he looked a lot older than my mom. He was big and tall, and he wore his long, light-colored hair back in a ponytail. He would peek in the door, without ever stepping foot inside. Sometimes, if he noticed me watching, he would give a little wave. But that was it. Jackson belonged only to my mom. He had no interest in getting to know me.

It took about a half hour before her headache felt better. Once it was gone, she got up, wrote a quick note to my teacher that I was late because I wasn't feeling well, and then I skateboarded to school.

Ten

Rose sat in the desk behind me. Ever since our fight back in fourth grade, I was careful to scrub my hair every morning so she couldn't tease me about being greasy. But she still ended up finding plenty of other things wrong with me.

"Why are you always late?" she whispered as I took my seat in our math class.

I didn't answer.

"Why were you late?" she tried again.

"I had to help my mom."

"Yeah, right."

I turned back to face her. I stared at her with the steadiest calm I could muster. She was as mean as she'd always been, but now that we were in sixth grade, she was pretty. "Rose, Rose, Rose," I sort of sang as I shook my head. If I let her have the last word, she'd win. And since I had nothing else to say, I just said her name.

She glared at me, then suddenly her expression changed to something that looked like panic. She started to blink uncontrollably. It was the most peculiar thing the way she was squeezing her eyes shut over and over like she couldn't stop. Quickly, she threw her hands up over her face as if to hide. "Stop looking at me, you freak!" she yelled through her hands.

I abruptly turned back to the front of the room. The teacher was now looking at us. "Carson Calley, stop bothering your classmates."

I sat there wondering what had suddenly happened. I could tell she was embarrassed. But it wasn't like her to get embarrassed. Especially by me. Something about this moment of vulnerability made me feel sorry for her.

I ripped off a corner of paper from my notebook and wrote, *I'm sorry, Rose.* Without turning around, I reached behind and set the paper on her desk.

A few moments later, she tossed another note back, all crumpled up. I unraveled it to find the words, *You ARE sorry Carson. You're a sorry loser.*

"Carson," came the teacher's voice. "Please bring that note to me."

I turned to Rose—my enemy and yet my partner in this crime. I found her blinking even more, apparently unable to stop. She hid her face again with her hands. There was no logic to my emotions, but I found myself feeling sorry for her again. I was like a dumb dog, faithful to my abusive master. I wanted to protect her. I grabbed the note I wrote from her desk, walked to the front of the room and only handed that note to the teacher. She wasn't too hard on me after seeing what I'd written. She just sent me back to my seat where I pretended the girl behind me, who remained hidden in her hands, didn't matter to me.

Eleven

I went back to Casper's place a little over a week after my last visit. There was no way of practicing confidence. I just had to go in one day and give it a shot. He gave me a second chance and that alone made me determined to make it work.

The "We'll be back in 20 minutes" sign was up and the door was locked. Casper sat on the beanbag while I kneeled before him.

When I healed my mom, I just held my hands over her, but I decided to try a few new things with Casper. I had him hold the turquoise stone against his heart as I put my hands up to his ears. Only one was bad, but I liked the symmetry of holding two hands on two ears. I made a faint buzzing sound in the back of my throat and small pressing motions with my hands. Coming up with a routine like that made it feel more legitimate. I pressed with a one-two rhythm, like a pulse, and Casper closed his eyes and relaxed into my care.

It was easier than I thought. I already had the power, I just had to say yes to it. When I said yes, I felt the thousands of tiny white stars pouring from my hands. I could feel the heat beneath my skin as the stars gathered and I knew the healing was about to begin.

I never completely understood where all the stars came from, but I thought it might have something to do with my attraction to light. It was like I fed off of it—and stored it like a battery. At night, I preferred to sleep with the lights on if my mom would let me. I had a continual urge to look up at the sun, though I resisted because my mom told me it could hurt my eyes. I loved watching fire, especially when my mom lit candles in the room. I craved car lights, brightly lit motel signs, sunlight, and even full moons. And sometimes when I didn't have an outside light, there was this light that seemed to come on inside of me. I could see it in my mind but I never knew exactly where it came from.

Sitting there with Casper, the stars continued to pour from my hands and I felt them going to his ears. I squeezed my eyes shut, focusing on gathering more and more stars, and then I just lost myself. I went somewhere deep and magical, and came out of it feeling exhausted.

"Wow," Casper said nearly a half hour later, when he put on music and set his ear to the speaker. "I think you did it. I'm serious. I think you healed me."

"Can you hear this?" I leaned in and asked directly into his bad side.

His eyes grew in amazement. "Yes!"

"You did?" I didn't mean to sound shocked.

"Yes. I haven't heard anything in that ear for years," he said getting up from the beanbag. He went to the wall and put his ear to it as he knocked. "I hear it!" He kept knocking and smiling. "You really are a healer. You are amazing, Carson."

I tried to keep a solemn expression on my face. I didn't want him to recognize how blown away I was that it actually worked. I wanted to keep up my confidence.

"We need to bring people into the shop so you can heal them." He was suddenly inspired. "It would be perfect here. I can help you start a healing practice."

"Maybe." I shrugged. "But I don't know if I'm ready for something like that yet," I said, walking around the glass counter as I eased my way to the door.

"I could help you. I could find the people, and take care of all the business, and you would just focus on healing." He followed me to the door.

"I guess we can talk about that next time, but I don't know right now if it's something I want to do, like a job."

"You show up here with this amazing ability—" his mouth was open and his hands were in the air. "You can't keep this gift to yourself."

"I know," I said opening the door. "I'll do it for more people one day. I just don't know about doing it right now."

He looked like he wanted to say more to convince me, but I quickly said goodbye and left.

I skated away from the shop and down the street toward the Vine. It was confirmed—I could heal someone other than my mom. With my mom, healing had almost become second nature. It just felt like that was my role in our relationship. It was routine. I could tell when she needed me, and I instinctively knew what to do. With Casper, the healing was different. He was someone new and much less familiar to me, and yet it still worked.

It wasn't that I didn't fully believe I'd healed Casper. I did. But on the way home I wanted to test it one more time, while my hands were still warm from Casper's session. I watched people around me on the sidewalk as I skated home and kept my eye out for some kind of injury. Just a block from our motel, I saw an old woman limping toward the bus stop. I wasn't sure how to approach her. I held my skateboard under my arm and watched her, thinking about what I might say. She noticed me and must have mistaken my staring.

"No steal from me." She narrowed her eyes and held her purse close with both arms.

"Oh, I don't want to steal from you," I said. "I just want to know why you're limping." I pointed to her leg. Her expression was like a question mark. So I mimicked her limp and then put my hands up like asking why.

She still stared at me, more curious than afraid now. "Bad," she said, patting her leg. "Car," she said, and then she pretended to slam her fist into her leg.

"You got hit by a car?"

She nodded. Since she barely spoke English I couldn't tell her I wanted to help her. It was probably better that way. What I was about to do wasn't the kind of thing you can put in words too easily. Especially to a stranger.

I went to the bus bench and patted the seat beside me. She came. I held my hands over her bad leg and closed my eyes. The stars came pouring out like they'd been building up in my hands, just waiting to be unleashed again. For the second time that night, the magic came through me. I felt like one of those superheroes on TV who walked around looking like a normal person until he turned on his gift. But a superhero was just a character. I was real.

When I finally opened my eyes and pulled my hands away, the old lady stood up. She took a couple steps and kept her eyes on me like I was a ghost or something. Then she bounced on her leg, and did a brisk walk down the sidewalk without a hint of a limp. She was halfway down the block when she howled what sounded like the long, last note of a sad song. She howled and howled, and I grabbed my skateboard and skated away. I didn't want to try and talk about it with her. Not only because she didn't speak English but because even if she did, I didn't know what to say.

That night, I lay in bed staring at the neon sign just outside our window. I felt exhausted, depleted. In some ways it was inspiring to realize I had that kind of power I could use on anyone. I bet every boy fantasizes about being a superhero sometime, and there I was almost like one. But in another way, it was scary. It felt like a lot of responsibility for someone who was just twelve. It was a lot of power to suddenly take on when I was more used to feeling small and powerless, like at school. What if people started coming into the head shop to see me and I didn't know what to do? What if I messed up and used my power wrong and ended up hurting someone? Truth was, I probably didn't even deserve the power I had. There was that other side of me no one knew about—the side that could go into a rage. Trying to manage both the power and the rage as a twelve-year-old felt like too much.

I wanted to ask my mom if it was okay for me to wait until I was an adult to be the healer I was meant to be. Maybe I could first grow up and then let my destiny happen. But my mom was already asleep. And since she had fallen asleep without drinking, I didn't want to take her away from one good night's sleep.

Twelve

The next morning, my mom wasn't as rested as I thought she'd be. I knew drinking was bad for her, but sometimes it seemed just as bad when she didn't get to have a drink.

"I don't know if I'm ready to be a healer." I decided to tell her at the table, even though she looked exhausted. I really needed to talk about it.

She took a sip of her coffee and looked at me across the table. "Why?" was all she said in a groggy voice.

"I just think it might be good for me to grow up first and be ready for that kind of power."

"You don't decide these things." Her voice was soft. "Your life was handed to you. You're part of a great plan. You can't back out of your role just because you think it's a good idea."

"But I don't know that much about it. I don't even know what's happening when I do it."

"That's the beauty of it. It's intuitive. It's real. You're not supposed to analyze it. You just feel it and you'll know what to do."

"Then can you take me to someone who knows about this stuff, just to kind of help me with it? I don't like not knowing anything."

She sat up a little straighter. "Maybe I can help you."

"But you're not a healer," I said. "You're a psychic. Aren't they totally different?"

She just shook her head a little.

"But how could a psychic help me with—"

"I'm the one who recognized your gift in the first place," she cut in abruptly, though her voice stayed soft. A deep breath gave her the strength to go on. "I explained everything to you when you were little. If I hadn't been there to give you direction, you might've just lost the gift altogether. So apparently I know something about healing."

"But do you think you know enough? I mean, enough to teach me what to do if I start using it on people?"

Both of her hands clutched her coffee cup. She lowered her eyes as she sipped. Setting the cup back down, she leaned her elbows on the table. With her chin resting on her hands, she said, "I'll take you to this woman I know—she comes to me for readings. She's a healer. She could help you take it to the next level."

My eyes widened. "Really?"

She smiled at my reaction. "I'll see if she'll spend time with you. She's a powerful lady," she said. "Her name is Lolo."

"I didn't know you did readings for a healer. I thought you only saw actors and actresses."

"Well." My mom squinted as she considered what I'd said. "She's a healer *and* an actress."

"Oh," I said. A healer who was also an actress—sounded kind of strange, but I figured in Hollywood everyone wanted to act, probably even healers.

My mom sat back in her chair. "I predicted her first big job on a commercial." She started twirling her hair around her finger as she gave me the beginnings of a smile. "I was the only one who knew she'd get it."

"So she'll probably do you a favor and see me?"

She nodded. "I think she will." She unwound the strand of hair from her finger and pressed her hands over her eyes. She looked miserable. Without a word, I got up and went behind her chair. Holding my hands out over her, I took away her misery. But just that day's misery. It always eventually came back.

Thirteen

It hurt a lot more than I thought it would. "You gotta stay still." Faris lowered his glasses and looked at me from above their black rims. He was sitting on a low stool, holding the tattoo machine with his left hand. "I'm good, but not good enough for a moving target. You understand?"

"Yeah," I said squeezing my fists and holding as still as I could.

"Okay then. Let's try again." It was the most serious and stern I'd ever seen Faris. I usually hung out with him when he was on a break, not when he worked.

The only sound between us was the light buzzing from the tattoo machine. Faris was completely immersed in his art, and I was totally focused on the pain. It felt like he was burning me. I had an urge to scream, or even just to moan, but I promised Faris I could totally handle it. Beans, the other tattoo artist, was at his station with a client, going through artwork. The place was small. They would have heard any noise I made. I held my breath until my face turned red and I felt lightheaded.

"You need a break?" Faris asked without looking at me. He dipped into the black ink and adjusted something on the machine.

A quick exhale rushed from my lips. "I'm okay," I breathed. That's when he looked up and noticed my face. He just nodded, and then brought the needle back to my skin.

The place usually smelled like sterilized metal. Faris prided himself on being one of the cleanest places in LA. But while I was getting the tattoo, I smelled ink and burned flesh.

To distract my mind from the pain, I looked around at the artwork hanging on the walls and on the partition that separated Faris' station from

Beans'. Their areas reflected their styles. Beans had sketches of funky skeletons and spooky-looking characters in his station. I heard Faris once tell a customer that Beans was into old-school Mexican art. The pictures were dark, but kind of playful at the same time.

In Faris' station there was a lot of war stuff hanging up—old guns, grenades, bomber planes. I was there once when a customer came in asking about a specific World War II gun and Faris pulled out a book to find photos of it. When I heard him talk to the guy, he seemed to really know his history. The two discussed the details of the gun and its significance in the war, and I was surprised at the intellectual conversation they were having. There was art and history in the making of that tattoo. I started thinking that for some people, tattoos weren't just about rebellion and looking cool.

Faris had another specialty—drawing women. From geishas to voluptuous naked ladies, he knew how to draw any kind of woman. When we sat outside the shop together, Faris loved to watch girls walking by, his eyes following them until they were out of sight. I figured he was good at drawing them since he studied them all the time.

The detail and the colors of all his tattoos were amazing. He was a real artist. I just wondered how he ended up choosing flesh as his canvas.

The buzzing stopped and Faris set the needle down. He grabbed a mirror and held it up for me. "Happy thirteenth birthday, " he said. Just below my shoulder, on the outside of my arm, was a small black crow with its wings slightly lifted, preparing to fly. I looked closely at the ink on my skin, the unerasable mark that would always remind me of the great man who could catch and kill a crow with his bare hands. I looked at Faris, not knowing what to say. It was the greatest gift I'd ever received.

"Now you got a permanent reminder that you came from good blood," Faris said.

"Yeah." I nodded. "Thanks, Faris."

"You sure your mom won't hassle me about this?"

I shook my head. "I told you, she thought it was a good idea," I lied. "She wanted me to have this in memory of my dad." I wasn't worried that my mom would get mad. I was pretty sure she wouldn't even notice.

"It's a good one—a damn good one. You know, this isn't my first black crow," he said, blotting off some blood and ink with a soft paper towel, then spraying alcohol on my arm. I almost squealed from the way it stung, so I tucked my lips between my teeth and bit down.

"I had a girl come in once asking for a crow on her back," he went on. "She said she'd just come out of a dark time in her life, and one of the things that got her through was all the crows around—she thought they were angels."

I briefly released my lips from between my teeth to ask, "Black angels?"

"No one said angels had to be white." He wiped at my raw skin, cleaning up the excess ink. "She was on the streets—maybe drugs, maybe homeless. I don't know, she didn't say why. But on the streets crows were everywhere. She said sometimes it seemed like they followed her, or surrounded her. Kind of eerie, but she came to see them as angels. You ever look at their wings?" he asked, putting Vaseline over the cleaned tattoo. "They really do look like angel wings—just black."

I looked down at the crow on my arm. My black crow. I could see what he meant. The wings did have an angelic quality to them. The ink wasn't even dry yet and my crow had already developed a new meaning for me. It wasn't just a symbol of my father's impressive power. I decided it also symbolized the angel that he was now, watching over me. It was an especially important time for him to be watching me as I was about to meet Lolo the healer and learn what I was supposed to do with my powers.

"You keep it covered for a while," Faris said. He put saran wrap over the tattoo and then walked me outside into the afternoon sun. Across the street, cops were breaking up another protest at the radio station. We sat together silently for a while, watching the chaos. It seemed to inhabit another world as I was filled with tranquility, sitting beside my friend with my new black crow etched into my skin.

For the first time, Faris shook my hand before I left. His grip was firm. My hand was smaller than his, but I tried to squeeze back. It lasted only a couple seconds, but there was something powerful about that brief moment. My mom never really seemed to notice that I was getting taller, and that I already had a little facial hair. My body was looking different, too. I figured she just didn't have the energy to pay attention to my physical development, and without a witness, it was hard for me to appreciate my own transformation. But now the day had come when Faris gave me a crow tattoo and a firm handshake. It was like he recognized I was on my way to becoming a man.

Fourteen

Visions and Dreamers, a metaphysical bookstore, sat between a shoe repair shop and a small Asian market, about a block down from the Pantages Theater on Hollywood Boulevard. My mom worked in a small room at the back of the little bookstore. The owner, a skinny, red-headed man named Nelson, had kept the door to the empty room bolted up for years because he thought an evil spirit lurked inside. When he placed an ad in the local newspaper looking for someone to remove the ghost, my mom responded. She assured Nelson that she was an expert in the field and asked for some time alone with the evil spirit to negotiate its departure.

My mom came home to me with this story when I was nine. Surprised, I told her I had no idea she was an expert on ghosts. She explained that if you're not afraid of them, you're an expert.

My mom had made Nelson promise not to open the door, no matter what he heard. He agreed and she entered the room, closing the door behind her. Despite the screams and banging sounds against the walls, Nelson stayed outside. After two hours, my mom came out of the room disheveled and exhausted. Nelson was in even worse shape—sweating and almost in tears.

"The spirit has requested that I come here at least twice a week," my mom told Nelson. "He has many issues to work on before he can successfully break through to the other side."

"He's stuck?" Nelson asked, shaking and clearly worried that the haunting wasn't over.

"Yes, that's exactly it. He's stuck. I've done work like this before. It's sort of like spirit therapy."

Nelson agreed to have her work with the ghost, and after only a month, it was healthy enough to move on. And just as the ghost finally moved out, my mom moved in. Nelson let her use the room for free to see her clients. In return, she would encourage her clients to purchase some of his books.

She'd been there ever since. That's where my mom got our books. Since I spent quite a bit of time alone at night in motel rooms, I read a lot. I didn't always understand the books my mom brought home, but all the topics were magical enough to keep me turning the pages. There was everything from books on mystics, witches, astrology, auras, and spirits, to stacks and stacks of tarot cards. I didn't know how to read the cards for the future, but my mom taught me how to make stories from them. Some nights, when I was tired of reading, I would create my own tales with the tarot cards. I'd arrange the deck all over the bed, imagining stories from the pictures.

I walked into the bookstore the day my mom took me to meet Lolo, and Nelson was standing beside a bookshelf. He was a small man. His red hair barely grew on his head, just mostly on the sides. He had a shiny bald spot above his forehead.

"Hi, Nelson," I said.

"Hello, Carson," he waved.

And that was it. Like Jackson, Nelson belonged only to my mom. She didn't want me getting close to him. We each belonged in different parts of her life. He was business. I was family. She kept the two separate.

My mom walked in front of me wearing a turquoise dress that looked like it was made of scarves. It was really short, revealing her long legs. Her cinnamon hair, barely brushed, fell well below her shoulders. It bounced along with her body as it moved. She looked like a cross between a gypsy and a retired supermodel. The way Nelson watched her, I bet he would have wanted her as a girlfriend if she didn't already have Jackson. I didn't like when she got that kind of attention from men. I sometimes wished she was more plain-looking.

My mom closed the door behind us. Sitting down on the lavender couch, I looked around the heavenly aqua room. There were pictures of gods and goddesses hanging on walls, angels, fairies, and clusters of candles set on shelves. It had always been a magical place to me. I felt an extra sense of magic in there that day as I prepared to meet my new mentor. My mom lit some candles and then knelt on the floor. She lit a smudge stick and we sat together in silence as the smoke cleared away the negative energy.

There was a light knock on the door before it opened. A brown face peeked in and smiled.

"Come in, Lolo," my mom said. The door fully opened and a large woman stepped inside and shut the door behind her. She wasn't fat, just solid with a lot more body than most people.

I recognized her immediately. She was the Islander who did the hula in that coconut soda commercial. It came on a lot when I watched sit-coms. "Drink the aloha!" she would call out as her grass skirt trembled with her fast-moving hips.

"It's good to meet you, Carson," she said, approaching me and sandwiching my pale, bony hand between her soft, plump ones.

"Good to meet you, too." I gave the appropriate reply with an inappropriate expression—disappointment. My mom hadn't told me I was going to meet the big coconut soda lady. I'd had this vision of my great healer mentor being a tiny, even emaciated old person with wrinkled skin and a solemn face. I think the idea came from my mom's stories about the old Native American healers from our past life. The ones she described were always bony, wrinkly, and serious. This lady looked too big, too young, and too cheerful to be a healer.

Lolo was quick to read me. "Don't let my abundant appearance fool you," she said, letting her hands travel down the sides of her big body, smoothing over her long blue and white hibiscus printed dress. It looked like she was wearing a tablecloth. "Healers come in all shapes and sizes. It's what's here," she pointed to her head, "and in here," she brought both hands to her heart, "that matter."

I swallowed, embarrassed that she'd read my thoughts, but her confidence didn't waver a bit.

"Your mom told me about the thousands of tiny stars that you feel coming from your hands," she said, lowering her body to the floor and sitting next to me. My mom got up and moved to the back wall, leaving us alone. "On the Island, my people call it *mauiamu*—the healing stars."

Suddenly, her size was irrelevant and her knowledge was all that mattered. This woman and her people actually had a word, a real word to define this thing I had inside of me. "*Mauiamu?*"

"Yes, *mauiamu*." She raised her hands with her palms facing me and then slowly and gracefully lowered them onto her lap. "And each little star that leaves your hand and travels into the person you are healing is a miraculous little morsel of energy that carries in it the ingredients of life."

"Does every healer have these stars in them?" I asked.

"No," she said with an unhurried shake of her head. "Very few people have the *mauiamu*. You are one of a special few in the entire world."

My eyebrows arched up. "Do you have it?"

"No," she admitted. "It was my grandmother who had the *mauiamu*. That's how I know about it. My healing powers are not so impressive. I can heal something that is broken, but you," she straightened up before informing me, "you have the power to give life to that which is dead."

I looked over by the door. My mom smiled and gave me an enthusiastic nod, but her expression didn't match the powerful impact of Lolo's words. My mom looked more frivolously proud—as if someone had just told me I had a nice singing voice.

I looked back at Lolo. "How does it work?"

"The life force from those stars has the power to revitalize the broken or dying cells in the body. So, say you have a blind man before you: you take your hands to his eyes and breathe." She inhaled deeply as she put her hands over my eyes. "Then you call forth the stars. You feel them surface from that special place deep within you, and they travel through your hands and into the blind man. Once you release the life force into his eyes, if his body accepts the energy, he will be healed."

Her hands were still covering my eyes, so I leaned to the side to peek at her. "What do you mean, if his body accepts the energy?"

She dropped her hands into her lap. "Healing is not a one-way street. You can only heal someone who is willing to receive the healing. But," she raised a finger, "that doesn't mean the person has to know you're healing him. He just has to *want* to be healed. You can send your energies to a stranger on the street and as long as he desires to be healed, your energy will be accepted."

"You said that I have the power to bring life to something that's dead." That idea stuck with me and I wanted to know more. "So what about a dead person. Do I actually have the power to bring a dead person back to life?"

"If you're like my grandmother, you do. When I was a little girl, I watched my grandma bring back a boy." Her voice was quiet and chilling, like she was telling a ghost story—but this was real. "He'd been dead for several years and my grandma made his spirit rise up from the grave and then his body came to meet his spirit."

"So she didn't even have to dig him up?"

Lolo shook her head, wearing an eerie smile.

"But was he all messed up from being dead so long? Like a zombie?"

"No, she had the rare power to lift life from the grave," she said, raising her palms toward the ceiling, "and make the boy come back as perfect as he'd been before he died."

My mom had a slight coughing fit over by the door. We both looked her way, but she just smiled and waved it off.

"But I think my grandma had something different from what you have," Lolo said, completely losing the ghost-story quality to her voice. "I don't think you were meant to do that kind of thing. Yours is the gift of healing people who are alive."

"But what if I do have what your grandma had? How would I know?"

"I think that's all the time we have," my mom called out from her perch against the back wall.

"But, Mom, we just started." I couldn't believe she was already bringing our meeting to a close.

"Lolo only had time to briefly meet you today," my mom said, walking to the candles and blowing them out. She flipped the overhead fluorescent lights back on. "But next time she can spend more time explaining things."

I looked to Lolo for confirmation. "Yes, I almost forgot. I have another appointment," she said, keeping her eyes on my mom.

"Carson, why don't you wait outside while I schedule your next session with Lolo."

I nodded. "Okay," I said. I knew something was up between them, but I also knew better than to argue with my mom. "Thanks, Lolo," I said, walking out of the room and closing the door. I didn't go outside but stayed next to the door and set my ear to it. I could hear muffled whispers. My mom sounded angry. All I heard her say were the words, "you went way too far," and, "it's dangerous—" but then Nelson interrupted my eavesdropping.

"Carson," he called out when he saw me. "Does your mother know you're listening?"

I shook my head and walked out the door.

On the way home, my mom and I didn't say a word to each other until we got to the front of our motel. That's when I found the courage to say, "Do you believe I can bring back the dead?"

My mom stopped and eyed me. I couldn't read her expression. Was it suspicion or concern? "Look, Lolo's a great person," she said, "but I honestly don't know where she's coming from with this bring-the-dead-back-to-life stuff. No one can do that."

"But if it's true, then what if I could actually help Dad?" I said, grabbing my right arm, just below my shoulder. "We could have him come back to us. And everything would be good again."

"You're a healer, not a god." My mom's eyes closed and she gave me a tired sigh. "You can't bring your dad back."

"Are you just afraid that it's dangerous for me to try?" I didn't want her to know I had eavesdropped, but I wanted to get the truth out of her.

"Forget about Lolo." She raised her voice now. "It was all a big mistake."

I stared at her.

"I tell her to help you and she manages to plant this crazy idea in your head." Her voice was quivering. "I need you to keep healing, Carson. I can't have you stopping now." She started shaking. She took a couple rapid breaths, and then a really deep one.

"Are you okay, Mom?" Her arms were trembling. It scared me. I reached out and tried to steady one of her arms, but she pulled away from me.

"I need to get out of here." She covered her face with her hands, and in her highest-pitched voice she cried, "I just need—I just need to get out of here."

"But, Mom," I said.

"Here," she fumbled through her purse for the key and then thrust it at me. "You go upstairs by yourself. I have to take care of something." She turned, still shaking, and rushed away.

"Mom, where are you going?" This wasn't good.

She didn't respond. She just kept walking. And I just watched.

Four days went by before I saw her again.

Fifteen

My mom had a way of wearing me out emotionally. Her love could be so comforting sometimes, but then it could be so confusing. Leaving me alone like that made me want to cry and punch in a wall at the same time. The first night she was gone I kept it together, but when she didn't come back the second night, I gave in to the rage.

Skating the streets, I came upon a little corner Italian restaurant that was closed. They'd left their statue out front—an almost life-sized chef wearing all white, with a big hat, and a red and white checkered apron. In one hand was a pizza and in the other a menu. There in the dark, with no traffic around, I pushed the pizza chef down like he was the one responsible for making my mom leave. I pounded him with my skateboard and with my hands. I kicked off his head and the pizza that he held. I beat him until he was destroyed—not repairable.

Skating away from the scene, I felt the same—not repairable.

The third night I didn't want to give in to the rage again. I was still feeling terribly guilty from the night before. I knew I needed to breathe deeply and stay calm. I needed to find a distraction so I wouldn't go out and do something bad again.

In an attempt to calm my aggression, I opened the drawer beside the bed and pulled out the Bible. I hoped to find inspiration on the thin, gold-rimmed pages that might calm and soothe me.

When I was around eight, my mom went through a phase where she started taking me to church. It only lasted a month or two. I liked the people there. They were always friendly to me. They talked about this beautiful place called heaven, and they spoke about how much God loved each one of us. I felt safe there, but one day my mom suddenly said we were done with them. "Religion is for people who aren't creative enough to come up with their own stories about why we're here," she explained to me.

"But you're the one who said we should go to church," I challenged her.

With a toss of her head and a careless laugh she said, "I had a brief lapse in creativity."

I always felt something magical when I listened to the reverend talk about heaven and the people who lived there. He'd once described the journey to heaven as going toward a bright light at the end of a tunnel. Sitting in church, I would close my eyes and take myself to that bright light he described. I imagined the light as massive as the sun and I felt a high as I took in its brilliance. I noticed other kids daydreaming and drifting off when the reverend spoke, but I was different that way. I was hungry for the stuff he talked about.

"I like their stories at church," I told her.

"But they're *their* stories," she said, "not yours. You need your own stories. I don't want you going through life just borrowing other people's ideas. You fill yourself up with too many of their beliefs, you won't have any room left for your own."

"But the other kids borrow the ideas, and their parents are okay with it."

Not only did I like listening to the reverend, I also liked the people at church. They were nice and they always served cookies and punch after every service—real homemade cookies that my mom couldn't make in a motel room. And every last Monday of the month they shared old toys and clothes with kids who didn't have many of their own. I wasn't about to let that all go so easily.

"You're not like other kids," she whispered. "I want you to look deep down in here," she put her hand up to my heart, "and find what the gods are telling you directly. They don't need to speak to you through someone else."

"But Reverend Tornow said that God already told people what he wants us to know when he had them write the Bible."

"You can find more wisdom in here," she said, now giving a gentle pat to my heart, "than in all the hundreds of pages of that Bible. That old book tells stories about people killing sheep to keep their god happy. How does that relate to you? Where the hell you gonna find sheep here in Hollywood?" She laughed a little at the thought.

"But could we still go back to visit sometimes?" I asked. I thought I'd be a little more specific and added, "Like the last Monday of the month?"

My mom smirked like she was onto me. "Well, I guess it wouldn't be so bad to stop in on a last Monday now and then. Maybe we could stay with the church just long enough to get a few more things for you."

"Thanks, Mom," I said. But we never went back to the church.

With my mom leaving me alone in the motel for a few nights after our argument, I thought maybe the comfort of someone else's story would help me escape the one my mom had written for us. Sitting on the bed, leaning against the pillows, I randomly turned to a page in what was called "The Book of Micah." I read it, but didn't really get it. I only knew that God sounded mad. Since I was trying to take the edge off of my own anger, I figured this wasn't the right story to turn to. So I tried another section, "The Book of Obadiah." It was the same kind of thing, though—God was really pissed off in that story, too. He was going to have one group of people burn up and devour another group. The story had a way of appealing to the rage growing inside of me, but that wasn't what I was looking for. I wanted to figure out which parts of the book had the God they talked about in church, the loving one—the one that might help calm me.

Feeling hungry, I set the Bible on the bed and went into the kitchenette. I cooked some Top Ramen noodles in the microwave and filled a drinking glass with sink water. Taking my dinner back into the bedroom, I set it on the nightstand and picked up the Bible again. Between bites, I gave the book one more shot.

I opened to a section that seemed to be full of poems. I read:

Oh, how I wish you would kiss me passionately!
For your lovemaking is more delightful than wine.

I thought this part could get good. Setting the book on the bed and leaving it open to that page, I reached for the Styrofoam cup from the nightstand. Holding it up to my mouth, I ate the noodles and drank the broth while I went on reading.

It ends up these lovers in the Bible *do it* somewhere outside in the foliage, under cedar trees and pine trees. I wondered if the reverend had ever read about these lovers in church. I remembered one lady my mom secretly called "Never-Been-Laid-Suzie." She always looked serious with her lips squeezed together and her nose up in the air. She would've been horrified if Reverend Tornow talked about *doing it* at all. The thought made me laugh there by myself in the quiet motel room, and for a moment, my heavy heart felt somewhat lighter, and that rage deep inside eased slightly.

After about fifteen minutes, I ended up sticking the Bible back inside the drawer, made myself a second cup of noodles, and turned on the TV. That Bible had some weird, random stuff in there. But my mom was wrong about it. Other people's stories *could* help, especially when your own weren't working out so well.

Sixteen

It was two in the morning on the fourth night that my mom finally came back. She was drunk, but an extra nice kind of drunk. She cried a lot, hugged me, and apologized for leaving. She told me she wouldn't do it again, but only if I promised that I wouldn't threaten to stop healing. I thought "threaten" was a weird word to use. I was just scared about using my powers on new people. I wasn't sure I was ready to heal strangers, but I didn't mean I'd stop healing my mom. That was how she took it, though.

"I got Lolo back," she said as her crying eased. She was sitting on the edge of my bed and running her fingers through my hair like she used to when I was little. "She's ready to teach you the right way to heal." Her words were only slightly slurred. "But no talk about the dead anymore, okay? That's not what you're meant to do."

I didn't want to tell her, but I thought she was wrong about that. I knew it was crazy to think I could bring my dead dad back to life, but wasn't it also kind of crazy to think I could heal Casper's deaf ear and the bus-stop lady's bad leg with invisible stars coming out of my hands? I wasn't ordinary. That was the one thing I knew for sure. And if I was going to be extraordinary, I might as well have extraordinary goals.

My secret plan was to learn all I could from Lolo, and then go to the Cemetery of Heroes in Washington DC and try to bring my dad back. I hadn't yet smoothed out all the details, like how I would pay for the trip, and then the most difficult part—how I would actually do it. I wasn't even positive I could do it, but if I was supposed to be the great healer of our time, I had to try to accomplish something that great. It made me look at my gift differently. I now had a reason to be courageous with it instead of afraid of it. Like my dad, I needed to find the courage to do something extremely difficult, maybe even dangerous, because it was heroic.

I woke up earlier than my mom the next morning. I went out to the side of the motel where ivy grew beside the walkway. Since I had been little, I'd known that ivy was a good place to find bugs, and I needed one for an experiment. Down on my knees, peeling away the green leaves, I passed up several spiders before catching a roach. I put it in the cleaned-out mayonnaise jar I'd brought. The roach scurried all over the glass jar as I carried it back to the motel.

Playing at a friend's house once, his high-school-age sister asked if we would help her catch bugs for her science project. She showed us how to put nail polish remover on a cotton ball and stick it in the jar with the bug to kill it. That way the bug wasn't smashed and she could pin it to a poster board and label it for her project. For my experiment that day, I also needed the bug not to be smashed.

Back in the room with my catch, my mom was still asleep. I went through her stuff and found nail polish remover, but no cotton balls. I used a wad of toilet paper instead, and tossed it in the jar. Once my roach stopped moving, I took it out and set it on the carpet. Holding my hands over the dead bug, I could feel my fingers warm up, and then the stars came flowing out. The energy I felt, even for just a roach, was powerful. I could tell something was happening.

When the little black creature suddenly twitched, I jumped back and watched, wide-eyed. I couldn't believe what I was seeing. Its movements were slow at first, as if dragging itself, but then the roach was up on its little legs, walking across the carpet. The dead had come back to life. I actually did it. In awe of my own power, I just watched the roach regain its strength as it wandered the room. I thought I'd be happy with my success, but something about giving the dead roach a second life felt eerie. Healing was satisfying—playing with life and death was kind of disturbing.

Out of nowhere came the scream, and then the shoe. I didn't realize my mom had gotten up to find me watching the roach roam our place. Her flip-flop came down hard on the resurrected creature and smashed it.

"Goddamn it, Carson," her voice was still groggy. "Why were you just watching it? Why didn't you step on it." That was when she noticed the jar, and took a couple sniffs of the air. "Nail polish remover? What are you doing?"

"I killed it with the nail polish remover, and then brought it back to life. Just before you stepped on it."

"Oh, God," she tossed her head back and rubbed her eyes.

"But it worked, Mom. Seriously. You saw it moving. I killed it and really brought it back to life." I hadn't planned on telling her about it, but once she witnessed it, I had to let her know.

"How long was it in the jar?" Her eyes rolled with the question.

"I don't know, like almost ten minutes."

She shook her head.

"Remember my friend Ricardo?" I said. "I used to play at his house in fourth grade? His sister did a bug experiment for her science class and she showed us how to kill the bugs. This was what she told us to do."

My mom walked away, leaving me to stare down at the crushed bug.

"You didn't kill it," she said coming back with toilet paper. She cleaned up the mess on the carpet. "You just stunted it."

"How do you know?"

"You have to keep it in the jar much longer to actually kill it," she said holding the crumpled up toilet paper out, away from her body. "We did that bug experiment back when I was in school. Some bugs were pinned down and started moving if they didn't actually die. A cockroach would take a long time to kill. A lot longer than ten minutes."

My mom took it to the bathroom and I could hear her flush it down. "Carson?" she called out. "Could you please leave the dead alone? Bugs, people, any kind of dead?"

"Okay," I said.

"Promise?" she came out folding her arms.

"Promise," I said looking away.

I didn't plan to do any more experimenting. Playing with life and death really did make me uncomfortable. I was fine with keeping ninety-nine percent of my promise to my mom. I'd only try it again when I got to my dad.

Seventeen

"She's back, huh?" Faris called to me while I was still walking toward the shop. I'd gone to see him the day before and told him how my mom hadn't come home.

"What, are you some kind of psychic or something?" I asked with my eyes all squinted up. I took a seat on the crate beside him. "How'd you know she came back?"

"I could see it in your walk," he smiled, setting his attention back on the protest across the street. "It's all body language—you're not dragging around like you were the last few days."

"Yeah," I admitted, surprised he knew. "She came back late last night, crying and apologizing." I pulled my feet up on the edge of the crate and rested my chin on my knees. "And drunk."

"Sometimes the bottle does that. Gets all those emotions out in the open, loud and clear."

"I'd say she was loud, but it wasn't all so clear to me."

He just nodded.

I wished I could have talked to him about my plan with my dad, but Faris wouldn't go for something like that. He didn't even really believe I was a healer. I told him about it, but I could tell he thought it was just a story. Faris wasn't real helpful when it came to the supernatural part of my life, but I was okay with that. He made up for it by being helpful in plenty of other ways.

We didn't say anything else to each other. We just kept quiet company as we watched the protesters at the radio station across the street. This time, there were girls lying on the sidewalk, all curled up and with fake blood on them. Maneuvering around the bloodied girls was an old lady in a wheelchair. A girl with dark hair pushed the wheelchair as the old lady shouted into a microphone with a portable speaker. She was talking in a harsh, threatening kind of voice. Her mouth was too close to the mike for all her words to be understood, but her tone was intimidating enough to scare you.

After a good ten minutes of watching the strangers across the street, the entire scene changed for me. Recognition clicked in my mind and I jumped up from the crate.

"That's her," I said pointing across the street.

"That's who?"

"That's the girl from school. Rose."

"Which one?" he leaned forward.

"The one pushing the old lady in the wheelchair."

He scanned the scene. Once he spotted her, he leaned back again. "At least she's not one of the girls on the ground," he commented. "That sidewalk is foul. I've seen homeless guys piss on it. A girl who would lie on homeless piss is one I'd stay away from." He gave off a grunt of a laugh, the way he always did when he was amused with himself.

"I wonder what she's doing there," I said, sitting back down on the very edge of the crate. "I didn't think she'd be into stuff like protests. She's too mean to care about anything but herself."

"I thought you liked her." Faris looked at me, narrowing his eyes.

"I don't know if I *like* her. I just said she was pretty."

"They have too much power over us, those hot ones," he said, lifting his shirt to reveal a curvaceous naked lady on the right side of his stomach. "This one treated me like crap and I stayed with her over five years." He let his shirt fall back over her, and dug in his pocket. He pulled out a cigarette.

I looked back across the street at Rose. There was something different about her. I was trying to get a sense of what it was when I remembered Faris' comment earlier about body language. I asked, "What can you tell about Rose from the way she walks?"

He took a moment to think about it, squinting as he watched her.

"She walks like she's pushing a heavy load," he said, sitting back and bringing his cigarette up to his lips.

"Well, obviously," I said. "But I mean not counting the wheelchair."

"I didn't count the wheelchair when I said it."

I just nodded, kind of getting what he meant. She definitely looked more insecure without her usual tough, snobby veneer. In fact, Rose seemed timid and maybe even embarrassed about being there. *That's probably why I didn't recognize her at first,* I thought and felt a twisted pleasure as I considered using that insight against her someday if she started in with me. I would tell her how I saw her at the protest and watched her push an old lady in a wheelchair. It would embarrass her, putting me in a better position next time she came up against me. I wondered if she felt the same kind of pleasure when she put me down. Maybe that's how it all started out between guys and girls, this little game of intimidation. Maybe it was just the natural beginning of two people liking each other.

"Do you think love has a mean side?" I suddenly asked Faris.

He smiled. "When you get your first taste of love and you start practicing what it is to love, yeah, it can be mean," he nodded. "But real love? Real love is never mean."

Surprisingly, his answer took my thoughts away from Rose and made me think about my mom. "But can't you love someone and sometimes be mean to them?"

"Well, sure," he said. "People are mean. But I'm just saying real love isn't mean."

The sudden loud noise across the street made us both jerk our heads toward the scene. The old lady with the microphone was screaming and this time the words were clear. "Murderers! Murderers! That's what you are!"

Rose, with her hands still on the back of the wheelchair, dropped her head and let her long black hair cover her face.

Eighteen

I was staring at her, but didn't realize she'd noticed. I wasn't looking at her eyes.

"Stop trying to look down my top, you perv!" Rose said. I was standing at my locker. Hers was just a few away from mine.

I was nervous about doing it, but here was my chance. "I saw you this weekend," I said. "You were at that protest at the radio station. I watched you push the old lady in the wheelchair. You didn't look too happy about it."

She looked surprised, but for only a second. "You *watched* me? You like just stood there and *watched* me? Creeper!"

"No, I was just—"

"Just a perv and a creeper," she cut me off. And then she started to blink rapidly. She was squeezing her eyes shut, then opening wide—squeezing and opening over and over. Before I could say another word, she turned and rushed away.

I stood there, dropping my chin all the way down to my chest. My plan had backfired. I thought I could embarrass her but instead, as usual, she managed to embarrass me. I wanted to leave right then, just skip the next class we had together. But I didn't. I gathered every ounce of courage I had and walked into the classroom where I would have to sit right in front of her.

To my relief, she ignored me for the first fifteen minutes. That's when I decided to pass a note to her and try to explain things. *I'm not a creeper. I was across the street sitting with my friend at his tattoo shop and I saw you. That's it.*

Her reply didn't take long. *Do you have a tattoo? R*

Now I had a major dilemma on my hands. If I admitted I had a tattoo, she might use it against me and tell on me. I could get in trouble and I bet I would get Faris in a lot of trouble since I was only thirteen. Yet there was the slightest possibility that having a tattoo might make her like me more. Rose seemed like the kind of girl who would like a guy with tattoos.

I took my pen and began to write my response, but then stopped. Instead, I leaned my shoulder back toward her desk, though still facing the front of the room, and lifted my T-shirt sleeve. I held the awkward position for a few seconds so she could see it for herself. That's when I felt her soft finger touch the tattoo. A chill rose inside of me, and my skin was covered with tiny bumps.

"I want a tattoo," she whispered into my ear. I'd never heard her voice sound so sweet.

"I can get you one," I offered, turning toward her.

She gave me a smile and her eyes went sort of lazy. "When?" School would be out the next week. This might give me a chance to see her over summer.

"Whenever," I said, wondering what was going on here between us.

The teacher looked our way, so I twisted myself back into my seat and kept my head down. Within a minute I felt Rose's hand on my shoulder, and then a folded piece of paper dropped into my lap.

Can you get me one when summer starts?

Just below her message I wrote, *I'll talk to my friend.*

In her next note she just wrote, *OK,* and drew a little heart at the bottom. I folded it and put it my pocket.

On my way home from school, I took the note out several times. I wanted to be sure it wasn't just a daydream. Rose really did draw a little heart for me.

Nineteen

Faris was in the shop giving someone a tattoo. I usually waited outside on the crate for him when he was working, but this time I wanted to see him right away.

"Car-son," he sang my name in greeting, looking up from his client.

"Hey, can I talk to you when you're done?" I asked, trying to hold back on the urgency I was feeling.

"You can talk right now if you don't mind saying what you gotta say in front of Pepper here." He motioned toward the girl standing before him. That's when I realized the girl was just wearing her panties, and a T-shirt pulled up and tucked through the V-neck. It was a lot of female body suddenly exposed to me—and just a few feet away. My eyes got stuck on the way her long legs, the color of honey, met up at that smooth space hidden under her panties. And just above her skimpy pink panties was a flat, honey-colored stomach with a tightly stretched belly button, and to the sides were the perfect curve of her hips.

It was her giggle that finally released my eyes from their grip on her midsection. "Hi, Carson," her sweet seductive voice teased me. Her face was really pretty but my eyes didn't stay there long. I looked back down at the exposed skin where her fresh tattoo was. Just above her hipbone was the profile of a bunny. Something made my eyes suddenly look up at her breasts, and then back to her panties. Everywhere my eyes traveled, I felt like I was peeking in on forbidden territory. I had to look away from her and over to Faris to get control of myself.

Faris' face held the deepest lines as his smile grew to a laugh.

"Uh, hi," I said to her. "I guess it can wait till you're done, Faris. I'll just—" I motioned to the back "—hang out over there."

That made them laugh even more.

I walked over to Beans, the other tattoo artist, who was looking through a magazine. He was a skinny guy with black hair that fell to his shoulders. He had a bunch of tattoos and piercings—a couple lip rings, a tongue ring, some that were stuck through his eyebrows, and piercings in his earlobes that had stretched out into big holes. He looked like a real rebel, but Faris told me he was twenty-five and still lived at home with his mom.

"Hey," I said, still rattled by my encounter with Pepper.

Beans looked up. "Carson, my man," he said. "What's going on?"

"I'm just waiting for Faris."

He looked over my shoulder at Faris and Pepper. "Yeah, Faris always takes his time with Pepper. Can't say I blame him. Shit," he said in a laugh, "Pepper is the finest woman ever to come into this shop." He shook his head. "I don't know how Faris does it. I couldn't give her a tattoo right there. I'd drop the needle if my hand was that close to her—" and he let out two whistles, a high one and a low one.

His words made me smile. I felt slightly less awkward knowing that she had the same effect on a grown man.

"When she leaves, I'll show you her shots in Playboy." My mouth dropped open. "That's right." Beans nudged me. "You're looking at a real live centerfold."

"No way." I looked back at her. She and Faris were laughing as he gently spread Vaseline over her tattoo. "No way," I repeated, still in awe.

"For real," he said.

I stood there beside Beans, staring over at Pepper. A Playboy bunny. I couldn't look away.

"Now all you need's a van with no windows, man," Beans said. "And a ski mask. And some duct tape."

"What?" I looked at him.

"You look like a stalker," he whispered, reaching for my shoulders and turning me away from her. "Just standing there staring like that."

"I just—" I shrugged.

"I know how it is," he said. "But you gotta get cre-a-tive." He moved his head side to side, in rhythm with the word. "Nothing wrong with staring if she don't know about it. But you gotta do it with dis-cre-tion." His head did that dance again.

He looked around the shop, and after some time he came up with the idea of having me sweep the place. It would get me close to Pepper, and if she caught me looking, I could just drop my head down real quick and pretend I was looking at the floor.

Beans handed me the broom, saying quietly, "Don't worry, man. It's the perfect cover." Beans was cool like that.

It did end up being a good cover. I managed to peek at Pepper quite a bit while I swept, and she didn't even look my way. Only when I heard her call out, "Goodbye, Carson," did I look right at her and wave. Once she left, I went to the window and watched her in her short shorts walk down the street.

As promised, Beans showed me Pepper's centerfold shots. My eyes got stuck on her again, just like they had earlier, until Faris made Beans put the magazine away. "Come on, Beans," Faris said. "I think the kid's seen enough for one day. We're corrupting a thirteen-year-old."

While Beans took the magazine back to his station, Faris motioned for me to meet him outside.

"So what was it you came to talk with me about?" Faris asked once we were out front. I'd almost forgotten about Rose after the whole Pepper situation. I sat back on the crate, leaning against the brick wall, and brought Rose back into mind.

"I was wondering." I set my eyes on the radio station across the street. It was quiet, no protesters. "Could I get you to give my friend a tattoo?"

"How old's your friend?" he laughed.

I hesitated. "Almost fourteen."

"Can't do it, Carson." His head shook.

"But you gave me one."

"You're like my own kid," he said. "And you cleared it with your mom."

"My friend won't tell anyone," I told him, even though I wasn't sure she wouldn't. I was feeling desperate enough to say anything.

"Doesn't matter."

"Seriously, she's gonna get one anyway, so why won't you just do it?"

"She." He laughed shaking his head. "Of course it's a girl."

"You gotta do this for me, Faris."

"There's no way I'm gonna do it." He was firm. "Might as well stop asking."

I swallowed and then looked away. This was bad. I hadn't considered what I'd do if he said no. The next week was our last week before summer break. I could skip the last days of school. My mom wouldn't know. And after school was over, I wouldn't see her until September. She'd probably forget all about it by then if I could just manage to avoid her. At least that's what I hoped.

"There'll be other girls," Faris finally said. "Lots of other girls. Who'll like you even if you can't do them a favor." I didn't say anything. Just kept my eyes on the street. "When I was your age, there was this girl named Victoria. Best-looking girl in school. She told me she'd kiss me if I'd erase her D out of our math teacher's grade book and pencil in a B for her."

"What'd you do?" I couldn't help but smile.

He threw his hands up. "Of course I *tried*," he said. "But I got caught."

"Did she still kiss you?"

"Hell no. She never talked to me again."

As I walked home, I wasn't thinking so much about Rose anymore. I was thinking about Faris. There was something he said early on in our conversation that kept popping up in my mind. *You're like my own kid.* There was no one else in my life who might say that to me. Faris was the closest thing I had to a dad. *You're like my own kid.* Those five words had the strangest effect on me that day. I stood taller than usual as I walked home. And I felt kind of important, like I really mattered to Faris.

Twenty

"'Imagination is more important than knowledge.' Albert Einstein." My mom's fingers released the quote and let it fall toward the cup, dangling from its string. "Mr. Einstein knew what he was talking about."

"Mm," I agreed with a full mouth. I was eating cold, leftover pasta my mom had brought home the night before from her dinner with Jackson.

My mom put both hands over her face and then slowly pushed them to the sides, stretching her skin as she went. Grabbing her hair just off her temples, she held tight so her eyes slanted upward. Her diamond earrings made a rare appearance from under her hair. "Who wants knowledge when we live in a world full of depressing truths?" she asked idly. "Imagination—that's what gets you through all the crap." She released her hair and let it fall to her face. "You create a beautiful world in your mind and then close your eyes, and you keep your eyes closed as you go along. Then you don't even notice the crap."

"You can't go through life with your eyes closed," I said, trying to twirl the unruly cold pasta onto my fork.

She gave me a look that wasn't at all motherly. "You're thirteen. You think you know more than me?"

"I'm just saying," I was careful with my response. I didn't like getting her mad.

"You have no idea what's in store for you in the real world once you become an adult," she said, leaning on the small table, her face up to mine. "You're still a kid, and I've protected you from some harsh realities. You've had mommy's hands covering your eyes to some of the crap and I'm telling you, once my hands get pulled away, you better close your eyes if you want to survive."

I stared back at her. I wasn't thinking so much about what she said—it didn't make sense to me anyway. I was thinking about how she said it with such a harsh tone. I couldn't tell if she was mad at me for something, or if she was just mad and taking it out on me. Either way, I didn't like it. My mom finally sat back in her chair and sipped at her tea. I tried to get back to my pasta but there was a cold silence there that made me lose my appetite. I set my fork down.

"We're meeting Lolo in thirty minutes," she said casually, as if she hadn't just gone off on me. "Will you be ready to go?"

"Yeah, I'll be ready," I said, getting up and taking the small Styrofoam to-go container to the trash. As I passed her, I slightly lifted the sleeve over my right arm, just below my shoulder. My black crow peeked out from my T-shirt. I walked slowly, giving her the chance to notice, but she never bothered to look up at me.

✻ ✻ ✻

My mom and I walked to the bookstore together with very few words between us. When we arrived, she stayed with Nelson and let me see Lolo alone.

The room was extra bright with the lights on as well as several candles lit. Lolo was sitting on the floor, her legs tucked under her, and her arms held up near her heart, as if in prayer. She wore another flowery dress, this one a soft yellow and white. Her dark frizzy hair was pulled up in a bun with yellow plumeria flowers surrounding it.

"Come," she invited me with a graceful wave of her hand. I obediently went to her and sat down. "Today, I will teach you a chant I learned from my grandmother." Her voice was different from the last time. She spoke with a slight Islander's accent. "If you begin your healing sessions with this chant, it will connect you to the wisdom inside of you, above you and around you. It will return you to your spiritual source. Listen carefully."

I was completely open to her, trusting her knowledge—though I was curious about her new accent.

But I pushed aside my doubts, and got caught up in her voice, deep and haunting as she began:

"E ho mai, ka ike mai luna mai e
O na mea huna no'eau, o na mele e
E ho mai
E ho mai
E ho mai"

Over and over she sang the chant as I tried to sing along and slowly learn every word. With just a song, that place of wisdom—inside me, above me, around me—was being revealed. As we sang the chant over and over, I felt almost numb to the world. I was all spirit, losing myself in the song.

When I had learned it without a mistake, we stopped singing. Lolo told me to sit quietly with my eyes closed, and breathe deeply. "You need to fully come back before I send you out the door. The chant has the power to take your spirit up high." I opened one eye to peek at her and her hands were raised up toward the ceiling. "But now it needs to come back down to your body so that you will leave here with everything together as it should be."

I took a few deep breaths and focused on getting myself back in one piece. My body felt light, like it might float to meet up with my spirit. I tried to squeeze my hands together but my muscles could only manage a gentle press. So I opened my hands up and let my body stay relaxed a while longer.

When I felt grounded again, I turned to Lolo. "Wow," I said, rubbing my fingers over my eyes. "How could a chant, I mean just a song, make me feel like that?"

"The rhythm of the chant allows you to harmonize with the vibrations of the Great Universal Spirit," she said getting up from the floor. "Most people only listen to the noise of the world, but they don't get in touch with the spiritual sounds—the ones that don't come down through our hearing," she placed her hands over her ears, "but enter here," her hands went to her heart. "You, Carson, connect more deeply with the vibrations than anyone I've ever known." Looking down at me she smiled.

"What about the light?" I asked. "Is there a reason I'm always drawn to light?"

She nodded. "Your mother said you would ask about that. She told me how you seem to crave light. I believe this is because you must feed from the light in order to fuel the *mauiamu*."

"What would happen if I didn't feed from outside light?" I asked. "Would the light that I see inside of me be enough?"

"You see it inside?" she gave me a surprised look.

"Am I not supposed to?"

She laughed a little and closed her eyes. She shook her head instead of giving me an answer, and I waited, watching her take deep breaths from her nose, exhaling through her lips. Her eyes stayed closed when she finally whispered, "I shouldn't be teaching you, Carson." She squeezed her lips, still not looking at me. She had dropped her accent when she said, "You should be teaching me."

"But I have another question." I swallowed before I went on. "Sometimes I can get real angry inside. Like angry enough to hit something." She didn't seem too shocked, so I went on. "It's like a rage building up inside of me and I want to do bad stuff." I didn't admit I did the stuff, I just told her how I felt. "It doesn't seem like a person who was born to be a healer would have that kind of bad inside of them."

"You're just a kid, Carson," she said, taking my hands. "You're going to have a lot of feelings inside of you while you're growing up and figuring life out. You're allowed to feel angry. It's okay to have those feelings, even if you are a healer. We all have them." I nodded to let her know I understood. "Maybe you can hit a pillow or something that won't hurt you. That might help get some of that built-up anger out of you."

"Okay," I said, wishing I could tell her that a pillow wasn't enough.

"Carson, I know your life can't be easy," she said. "I promise you, you're doing great for what you've got."

Twenty-one

I finally went back to the head shop to see Casper. It had been over a month and a half since I'd healed his ear. When I walked in he was carrying a couple of brown boxes to the counter.

"Carson," he smiled, surprised to see me.

"Hey, Casper."

"I'm sorry," he said right away, bowing his head and letting his pale dreads fall toward his face. "I didn't mean to scare you off last time with all my talk about starting a healing practice here. I was just so excited that you really healed me and thrilled to have found you. I wanted to share you with the world. But if you're not comfortable yet, I totally understand."

"About that," I tapped my finger on the glass counter as I spoke. "I was thinking—would we charge the people?"

My desire to heal wasn't motivated by money—it was much deeper than that. But I did need to make some money to buy an airplane ticket to Washington DC. And then I'd need enough money to fly both my dad and me home if it all worked out.

"Yes, of course." Casper's eyes lit up. "You think you might want to do it?"

"I could try."

"I will set up the back room for you." He smiled and clasped his hands together. "And I will take care of bringing people in. All you have to do is heal, Carson. I will take care of everything else."

"Once I save up enough money, I wondered if you could do something for me."

"Of course," he said.

"Would you help me buy a ticket to Washington DC so I could go visit my dad?"

"Is that where your dad lives?" His eyes widened.

"Yeah, that's where he is. And I want to surprise him." I didn't make lying a practice, but it came easier to me than I thought it would.

"That would be a wonderful surprise, Carson. I will look into costs for you and I will take care of getting your ticket." He grabbed a pad and paper. "Washington DC ticket for Carson," he said as he wrote. "Has he lived in Washington DC for very long?"

"Pretty long," I said. "Where's your dad live?" I quickly asked, not wanting to lie anymore than I had to.

"My father and mother live in Seattle. Ben and Diana." He smiled as he said their names.

"Your real name isn't Casper, is it?"

"No," he laughed. "My real name is Benjamin Dampleson. Casper came from all the teasing at school." He lifted his poncho's long sleeve to reveal his pale skin. "And the name stuck. My parents would have never given me a playful name like that."

"Why not?"

"They were too serious. Both college professors. They were quite strict raising me." His eyes went upward as if recalling his childhood. "They'd only let me watch educational TV, I had to read a book a month, and before taking vacations we had to study the geography as well as sociology of our destination." He looked back down at me with a smile. "You get the idea."

I nodded. Now that he was into his story, I could tell I was safe from him asking anymore questions about my dad. I made my way around the counter and sat on the beanbag beneath him to hear the rest.

"I wasn't wired like my parents. After high school, I moved here to LA to find a new kind of life. I was immediately drawn to the Rastafarian culture." He put his hands out toward the merchandise around the store. "I didn't look very Rastafarian—until I grew my dreads, but it is such a kind and accepting group, the owner of the head shop hired me anyway. My father didn't like that though. He didn't want me working as a simple employee at a head shop. So, long story short, he bought the place for me."

"This shop is yours?" My mouth fell open. "You actually own it?"

"Yes. My father thought owning this place would be more respectable than just being a minimum wage employee here. And it's worked out for me. I have the freedom to run things however I want to."

Casper went on and on with his story, telling me about the last two years running the head shop. I stayed on the beanbag listening to it all while watching him unload a box of essential oils into the glass cabinet. I read some of the little bottles as he set them on the shelf—patchouli, sandalwood, cinnamon, lavender. He kept on talking even when he went to the back to grab a small clay bowl that had a candle underneath. Setting the bowl on the counter, he poured a few drops of patchouli oil into it. He lit the candle beneath, and the earthy smell filled the room.

When his story made it to the present, he told me that the greatest success of the shop would come from me and my healing. "Come here," he said walking toward the back of the shop and waving for me to follow. "I want to show you something."

I got up from the beanbag and followed him to a door, down the hall just before the bathroom. He opened it and I looked inside.

"This is where I'll set everything up for you." He smiled. "This is your room."

Inside was an almost completely bare room that had white walls, a bright light bulb hanging from the ceiling with no cover, and a few boxes off in a corner. It didn't look like anything special, but the small space inside those white walls was going to be mine. That made it feel special. "You don't need to use it for anything else?" I asked, walking in further. I put my hands out like I was feeling the space.

"Nothing could be more important than what you're going to do," he said. I looked back at him in the doorway. He stood there with his hands in the pockets of his poncho. "I feel like I've been given a responsibility with you. Here you are, this magical boy, and no one knows about you. Your gift isn't something you should be hiding, or keeping to yourself. It's something you need to share with the world." He came to me there in the middle of the room and put a hand on my shoulder. I could smell the patchouli oil on his hand. "You're too young to do it all on your own, so I'm here to help you."

"But why do you want to help me?"

"One, I don't believe in coincidences," he said, lowering his eyes, his white lashes sort of fluttering. "I think you came to me for a reason and I can't ignore that. Two," he said, looking back up at me. "This will give new direction to the shop's business. I think you could be a great success here and that would benefit us both."

I was mostly looking for a way to make some cash to go see my dad, but Casper had me inspired. "Maybe it is more than a coincidence," I said, thinking about how unlikely it was to find someone who would want to help me start up a healing practice. My mom's prophesy came to mind, when she told me at ten that I would become the great healer of our time. "Maybe this is how it's supposed to start," I said.

Twenty-two

My mom seemed to have crawled deep inside herself. She barely talked to me during the day. I still heard her stories when she came home late at night, though she didn't incorporate me into them anymore. Our past lives were gone from her mind—even the present life we shared was of little concern to her. She rarely asked me to heal her. She started drinking a lot more and I wondered if she was so far gone she didn't even feel the pain anymore. She would just come home, crawl into the twin bed across from mine, and wake me up with the loud retelling of the night's dramas. They were almost always about Jackson. With those late-night stories, I learned more than I needed to know.

It ends up the guy was married. She had been trying to create a family with a man who already had his own family. And I learned that our living in motels all those years had not been a necessity. Jackson had been giving her plenty of money for a place (my mom threatened to tell his wife if he didn't), but my mom chose motels over an apartment so that Jackson would recognize her living arrangements were temporary. An apartment would appear too stable, and even permanent. She wanted to make it clear to him that she was waiting.

"Waiting? For like ten years?" I asked her, shocked.

"Love has no time limitations," she slurred the last word.

Jackson tried to keep her satisfied with the way things were by buying her jewelry and taking her out to fancy restaurants. I only wished she had asked him for a few extras over the years that could have benefited me as well.

I didn't know what to do with the new information. It felt like a huge betrayal. I quietly resented her and kept focused on my journey to see my father.

I was tired of being alone every night, just waiting in the motel until my mom got back. I started going out at night, skateboarding down Vine, heading toward Hollywood Boulevard where I'd hook up with some new friends I'd met on the streets. There were about ten of us, ranging in ages from eleven to seventeen. We'd meet in front of the Henry Fonda Theater where Buddy, a skinny kid with a shaved head, would bring a wooden skate ramp and a jar for tips. We'd take turns doing jumps off the ramp while people in line for concerts at the Fonda would throw change, and sometimes even dollars, in the jar.

Some nights it felt like such a rush skating the lit-up streets of LA, the cool air biting my skin, freedom launching me off the wooden ramp, and then the applause of strangers coming at me once I'd landed. I felt like part of a team, connecting with the other skaters whose hearts were beating just as fast mine, and whose T-shirts were as sweat-soaked as mine. We didn't talk much to each other. The group's connection didn't come from words. It came from a common vibe, a common need, a collective loneliness temporarily abated on Hollywood's sidewalks.

When the line of people would disappear into the theater, we'd skate off together to a dark neighborhood away from the busy streets. Buddy would take some of the money from the tip jar inside the old building with the address 1111 crookedly set above the front door. The rest of us would wait outside, keeping our eyes on the seedy people who hung out around the apartments. Agitation would keep us skating there in front of the building until Buddy made it outside with the bag of goods. Then we'd storm out of the dark neighborhood and skate back to a deserted parking lot just behind the Fonda.

We stayed hidden behind a dumpster there in the lot, clumped together in the small space like a litter of stray kittens. Some of the older guys would get high with Buddy, while the younger ones would goof off like little brothers, happy to be part of the gang. I stayed with the younger ones. No one cared if I got high or not. They offered it to everyone, but didn't pressure anyone. Weed was too expensive to waste on someone who didn't really want it.

The first time it was offered to me, five of the guys were smoking together in a circle, and three of us were off in front of the dumpster. The smallest kid, Cooper, had climbed inside the dumpster and brought out a lady's purse. He emptied it onto the ground and we grabbed at the stuff, wrestling each other for it, and messing around with it all. The other kid with us, Boone, found breath spray in the purse and aimed it at our faces. It was like a rush of mint up my nose, but it stung my eyes. I grabbed it from him and threw it far off into the dark somewhere. We moved on to the lipsticks from the makeup bag, and wrote on the dumpster, cracking up at our lipstick graffiti—hot pink, dirty words. It was when Cooper launched a tampon over to the circle of smokers that they even paid any attention to us.

"Grow up," one voice called out.

"Stick it up your ass," another said, making us laugh. Somehow things were extra funny late at night hanging out with my friends. I bent over, laughing harder than anyone.

When I looked up I noticed Buddy watching me. "Carson? You wanna try?" he asked, holding up the joint. There was still a smile on my face from laughing, but the smile froze as I considered how he might react to my answer.

I knew I didn't want to try it. I'd already thought about it. I saw what alcohol did to my mom, and what those mushrooms did to Casper's ear. I didn't want to mess myself up. If I was to be a great healer one day, I needed to take care of myself. But it wasn't just about the future. I had the present in mind, too. I wanted to be someone my dad would be proud of, especially if I could bring him back home. But right then, at that moment, it wasn't about being a healer, or making my dad proud. It was about hanging onto my friends. I didn't know if Buddy would get mad at me for saying no. What if refusing him meant I couldn't hang out with them anymore?

I gave him my answer quickly. "No, thanks," I said. I was afraid that Buddy had heard how awkward the words came out, how my voice cracked a little. But he didn't. Without a word, or even a look, he just turned back around to his group. He didn't care. Relieved, I felt like laughing again, and Cooper and Boone—for no apparent reason—laughed along with me.

The three of us went back to the dumpster where we made Cooper climb back in to see what else he could find. The older guys just stayed in their circle, doing whatever it was they did when they were high. Eventually flashing lights and sirens headed toward the lot. We all got on our skateboards, riding off in all different directions, heading home.

Twenty-three

Casper fixed up the back room, painting the walls light turquoise, and covering the floors with warm, earthy throw rugs. The bare light bulb was replaced with an orange stained-glass ceiling fixture he'd found at a garage sale. The shelves along the walls were stacked with candles of every size and color. There were no couches or chairs, just a stack of Mexican blankets in the corner—colorful, striped, handmade ones that Casper had picked up on a weekend trip to Tijuana. People coming to see me would choose a blanket, take it to the center of the room, and sit on it. I would then sit facing them on my own blanket.

I showed up at the head shop one early July morning and she was already there. She was barely five feet tall, petite in stature, and yet she seemed to take up a lot of space in the room. Her name was Harper Dee and she was the lead singer of an indie rock band. She wore black spandex pants that went to her knees, a black spandex tank top, and red Converse shoes. She had dark, straight hair that loosely framed her face. Sulky lips, dreamy eyes, and a little girl's nose—she was cute and beautiful at the same time.

"You're just a kid." Her voice was raspy, her smile mellow as she looked me over. "How's a kid gonna heal me?" She looked to Casper.

"This boy here is miraculous," Casper said. "He has a rare gift that defies his age. You will see." Casper had a way of speaking that made you believe he was telling the truth.

"Well, then, Carson." She cleared her hoarse voice as she brought her hand to her throat—black and silver bracelets climbed her arm, silver rings circled her fingers. "Think you can come up with a miracle to help me get my voice back for tomorrow night?"

"The back room is all ready for you," Casper motioned toward the back of the store with his hand. He had a couple twenties held between his fingers.

I was exhausted. The night before, we had made more money in the tip jar than usual. Buddy got pretty wasted on all the stuff he was able to buy, and ended up passing out behind the dumpster. A couple of the other guys and I had to set his dead weight on a skateboard and maneuver him home. He threw up most of the night and I was the one who stayed to take care of him. I was familiar with that kind of thing. I stood there before the indie rock singer, after getting barely four hours of sleep, feeling a bit zoned out.

"Well—do you think you can help me?" she asked.

I wiped my tired eyes and took a deep breath. I wiggled my fingers and tried to feel the sensation of the tiny stars in them. With a flush of sudden inspiration going through me, I felt the stars gathering up.

"Yes," I said confidently. "I *know* I can help you." One hundred percent confidence, just like my mom said.

Harper chose the Mexican blanket that was mostly black and red. She spread the whole thing out, and instead of sitting on it and facing me, she lay down on it. I adjusted to her way. I sat behind her head, my legs folded, and reached my hands out over her throat. As I chanted, Harper hummed along with me. The stars flowed out in rhythm with our voices. I felt her spirit. It was so easy to connect with her. After some time, we were completely in a zone together and she wasn't humming anymore—she was singing along with me. She knew all the words.

When her voice fully came back, I closed my lips and let her sing the chant solo. Hers was the most exceptional voice I'd ever heard. She altered the rhythm a bit as she got up from the floor. Still singing, she took my hands and led me in a dance. I'd never danced with a girl before, unless you count the times my mom danced around with me as a kid. I felt awkward at first, but I noticed she kept her eyes closed. So I figured it was safe enough to let my body follow her swaying hips and her flowing arms. It was spiritual yet funky—soothing yet wild.

Harper transitioned into other songs that sounded like they were probably her originals. I got caught up in dancing and she kept singing. I felt freedom there in the turquoise room, moving my body to her music. It was like letting out feelings without saying a word. One song was full of rage and she took her voice up to a scream at one point. I let my body move with more force, feeling everything she said.

The last song was a slow quiet one. She came to me and put her arms around me. I put mine around her. Somehow it wasn't embarrassing at all. We were both a little sweaty, but it was okay. She sang about acceptance and understanding, more like a love song for the world instead of just love between one guy and one girl. I felt what she was saying, not only in her words, but in the way her voice vibrated into my body. And I understood.

Before she left, she gave me one of her CDs. I put it in the CD player and replayed all her songs once she was gone, trying to hang onto the moment we had just shared.

Twenty-four

It was morning but my mom still seemed drunk. "Shit," I heard her say following a loud crash. I came out from the bathroom to see what had happened. "I can't get it together this morning, Carson," she said, trying to tip-toe over the broken glass. An empty wine bottle from the night before lay in pieces on the floor of the kitchenette. Her arms flew up as she tried balancing on her toes, maneuvering her way around the shards. When she made it out, she grabbed her hair, pulled it behind her, and held her forearms at her temples, like she was squeezing her head. "Honey—" she shook her head without looking at me "—why don't you go ahead and meet Lolo by yourself today. I don't want to make you late and I gotta clean up this mess."

"You want me to help you?" I asked.

"No," she looked at me and gave me a tired smile. "You go be a healer, honey."

I finished getting dressed while my mom climbed right back into bed. Before I left, I swept up the broken bottle.

"Bye, Mom," I called out from the door.

"Could you do me a favor?" she called back. "Tell Nelson to reschedule anyone who comes in today. Tell him I'm at a psychic seminar."

The way my mom lied so easily, having me tell Nelson she was at a psychic seminar instead of home in bed with a hangover, made me question her. Did she ever lie to me? I knew she exaggerated sometimes. I could tell she added details to some of her stories, but I didn't want to believe she would ever outright lie to me.

When I walked into the backroom of the bookstore, I asked Lolo if we could light a smudge stick before our session. It took some time to clear away the negative energy that day, but Lolo was patient. Once it was cleared, we started our routine.

"*E ho mai*," Lolo began with that deep haunting sound as I knelt on the floor beside her. "*Ka ike mai luna mai e,*" I joined in. "*O na mea huna no'eau, o na mele e.*" Our combined voices grew into an essence of its own—a presence there in the room, with us and yet separate from us. It called on that place of wisdom—inside of us, above us, around us. "*E ho mai, e ho mai, e ho mai.*" And that place of wisdom was revealed.

Again and again we sang the chant. I lost myself in the vibrations. My eyes latched onto the flickering candles. It fed the fire inside of me. I felt the power. I felt my destiny.

It was great while it lasted, but when our session was over, I dropped back down to the real world. That wasn't as great.

"Something's wrong with you. I can tell," Lolo said when we turned the lights back on.

"Well." I figured it was safe opening up to her. "Sometimes I don't get my mom. You know how she is." I rolled my eyes. "Sometimes I even wonder if I should trust all the things she tells me."

Lolo just stared at me for a moment. "Your mother has her own spirit issues to deal with. I know how she can be sometimes," she said, letting her eyelids drop. Her head nodded slowly, and when she looked back up at me she wore an apologetic smile. "But don't ever question yourself or your gift, Carson. You have something very special in you. Never doubt that. Even when it feels like you have reason to doubt everyone else, never doubt yourself. Okay?" She waited for me to reply.

"Okay," I said. "Lolo? Could I just ask you one question about bringing back the dead?"

"Carson." She shook her head. "Your mom said we can't."

"But could you just tell me if it's any different than the way I give the stars to someone who's sick?"

"I really don't know." She wore a pained smile. "I can't teach you about that."

"But then just tell me this. Is it true that it's dangerous? If I stand over a grave, and just try to bring someone back, is there anything dangerous about that?"

She looked at me, with her lips pressed together, like she was holding back a secret. "Okay, Carson, it's not dangerous," she finally said. "There's no danger in it because it won't work. It just won't work."

After our session, I skated to the head shop only thinking about one of the things she'd said—it's not dangerous. That was the only part that mattered to me. I knew I could do things that ordinary people couldn't do. Adults didn't usually believe me. Neighbors at our motels and some of my teachers thought I was lying to them when I said I healed my mom. One teacher even sent me to the school counselor, claiming I was confusing reality and make-believe. The school counselor tried to convince me that being a healer was only make-believe. That was when my mom told me to keep my healing stories to myself. She explained to me that people couldn't always understand what they didn't know how to do themselves.

"Sometimes," my mom said, "it's better to keep all your truths inside so the doubters don't get you to stop believing in yourself. You know what's inside better than anyone else ever could."

I believed her back then, and at thirteen, I still believed. I knew what was inside of me better than anyone else could.

After a full day of healing at the head shop, I skated back to the motel but my mom was already gone. I ate some crackers on the counter and then I skated over to the Fonda to meet up with Buddy and the guys.

Twenty-five

"You disappeared for a while." Faris greeted me with his old wrinkled smile as I approached the shop. He was sitting in his usual spot. "Thought I was gonna have to come looking for you."

I stood next to him and looked across the street. "Just been busy."

"Yeah, doin' what? It's summer."

My mom was either too preoccupied or too drunk to ask me about my life, but Faris was the kind of guy who asked questions. He paid attention to what I was doing, making sure I stayed out of trouble. If he knew I spent my time with guys that got high, he'd have something to say. Faris had a way of knowing things about me even when I didn't tell him. I stayed away for a while so he wouldn't figure it out.

"I'm working," I said leaning up against the crate, but not quite sitting down.

"Where'd you find a job?"

"Casper let's me use a back room at the head shop and I've been getting paid to heal people. Remember I told you that he was gonna set the room up for me?"

"Yeah, I remember," he said with a nod and a scratch to his chin. I watched the jagged lines and Chinese symbols on his fingers dance along with the movements. "How does he pay you?"

"We split everything fifty-fifty," I said.

"You okay with the arrangement?"

"Yeah, it's fair." I wouldn't know how to get the business on my own anyway, so I was fine splitting it with him.

"How's it going so far?"

"I think I'm pretty good at it. I mean I haven't seen that many people yet, but I healed all the ones I did see."

"Mm," he said. He never had much to say when I talked about my healing. "What else you doing with your time?" he asked.

"Skating. Hanging out with friends." My eyes darted toward him to see if he was going to question what kind of friends. He didn't. He just lit a cigarette and kept his eyes on the street.

"That girl came here asking about you," he said after a little while.

"Rose? The girl pushing the wheelchair?" I pushed forward off the crate almost losing my balance.

Faris just nodded, giving me a knowing smile.

"What'd she say?"

"Asked if I'm the one who gave Carson Calley his black crow tattoo."

"Did you tell her?"

"Told her she'd have to ask Carson Calley."

"Then what'd she say?" I practically shouted.

He folded his arms. "She asked where she could find you."

"And?"

He shrugged. "Told her I haven't seen you in a while."

"Stop messing with me, Faris. Just tell me what happened."

"She wanted me to give this to you." He pulled a note from his pocket and handed it to me. It had an address, 714 West Cherry, and it said: "This is where I babysit Mondays and Wednesdays from 8 to 5."

"So what am I supposed to do?" I asked.

"Well, if you like the girl, you go to that address on a Monday or a Wednesday. If you don't like the girl, you don't go."

"What if I like the girl, but I'm afraid of her?"

That made Faris laugh. "We're all afraid of them in the beginning," he said. "You know what, scratch what I said before. Here's my new advice: whether you like her or not, go to that address. You need some experience dealing with girls. And I'm guessing that if you can survive this one, you'll be in good shape when you meet yourself a nice girl."

Twenty-six

A five-week-old baby with pneumonia came into the head shop one morning. The doctors had put him on antibiotics for ten days and he still wasn't getting better. The baby cried and screamed, his tiny voice sounding hoarse and weak. His distraught mother clutched him close as she sat on a Mexican blanket in the middle of the turquoise room. I sat facing her, candles along the periphery of the room giving us light.

"I heard about you from my neighbor," she spoke as she bounced the crying baby. "She said you were young, but my god. How old *are* you?"

"Thirteen."

We'd been getting the same reaction over and over. People would meet me and grow skeptical because of my age. They'd look from the quirky albino with the dreadlocks to the small-for-his-age thirteen-year-old and wonder if this was some kind of scam. I didn't try to convince them I was real. I just showed those who stayed long enough that I could really heal them.

"I mean I'll give you a chance," she said, more desperate than hopeful. "Just try something."

I squeezed my hands into fists and then let them go limp. I cast my eyes on a candle against the wall and took in the light. At first I felt slightly uncertain. Lolo had told me that healing is not a one-way act. I could only help someone who was willing to receive the healing. Was this infant even capable of being willing to receive my healing? As the baby screamed louder, his mom began to cry along with him. Her eyes clung to me. They were helpless and desperate. I was certain *she* was willing to receive the healing, so I had an idea.

"*E ho mai,*" I began to chant with one hand over the baby and one hand toward the mom. I conjured up the thousands of tiny stars and let them spill over the two of them. With the purest of hearts, I gave and gave and gave them the light. I found myself looking from candle to candle to candle, drawing light from each one, feeling the heat travel through my body. It wasn't only my hands that felt it. The warmth seemed to have reached my blood, and it moved along inside of me. I started feeling feverish, even a little weak, but I had to keep giving. I'd wondered if I was coming down with something when I woke up that morning—my head a little stuffy, my body a little achy. This session seemed to be further depleting my body of its strength.

The mom began to calm first. She had stopped crying and eventually started breathing slowly. Her hand gently caressed the baby's arm, and soon, the baby's cries stopped as well. I couldn't tell if he had responded to me, or to his mother, but there was no doubt that he was responding to the moment. Once they had both calmed, I couldn't take my hands away from them. The peace that had washed over this mother and child made my feverish state feel exhilarating despite the physical discomfort. I had a feeling I would be sick later, but nothing mattered more than staying with the heat that brought on the stars. I was willing to give my whole self to healing the child.

The baby was healed. The mother was happy. And I was definitely sick. I didn't even have the energy to get excited over Casper telling me that we almost had enough money to buy my plane ticket to Washington DC.

I went back to the motel and my mom hadn't gone out yet. I must have looked terrible because she actually noticed. Putting her hand over my forehead, she said, "You're burning up. You probably have the flu I had last week."

"You had the flu?" I asked.

"Don't you remember me throwing up?" she said.

I didn't even answer her. There was nothing unusual about that. What was unusual was my mom's concern. She stayed home that night to take care of me, only leaving briefly to go to the store. She went to pick up a bottle of Tylenol for me, and a bottle of wine for her. She watched TV from her twin bed, occasionally getting up to put a cold towel on my forehead. I was pretty out of it, but I kept opening one eye, while laying on my pillow, to see if she was still there. She stayed all night.

The next morning she brought toast and a cup of herbal tea to my bed. She took eucalyptus oil and massaged my shoulders and neck. It felt like when I was little, the way she took care of me.

"You want me to go get some of that soup from Susie's?" she asked. Susie's was a health food café my mom sometimes sent me to when she felt really sick the next morning.

"Sure," I said.

She kept looking at me like she wanted to say something, but the words never came out. Instead, she came over to my pillow, and with her hands on the sides of my head, she leaned down to kiss my forehead. Then she left to get me soup.

Twenty-seven

There was a line outside when I got to the head shop. It looked like Casper had some kind of sale going on. People watched me as I walked to the front of the line and all eyes were on me when I was about to go inside. It seemed like they had the wrong idea. "I'm not cutting in line," I let them know. "I work here."

That brought on some laughter from the crowd, but I didn't know why. I slid through the door and made my way through the people inside. "Why are so many people here?" I asked when I got behind the counter.

"They're all here to schedule an appointment with—" he put his hands out as if presenting me "—the Hollywood Healer." Those inside began to applaud.

"How old are you?" a guy back by the door called out.

"Is it true that you can even heal cancer?" a lady's voice called out.

My heart started racing. I'd never spoken in front of a group like that except once at school when I had to present an art project to the class. I used matchbooks I'd taken from the motel's storage closet to make a house. All the kids laughed at me and the teacher sent me to the principal for bringing matches to school.

Casper must have noticed how scared I looked. He asked everyone to hang on while he took me to the back. "Are you okay?"

"I don't like talking in front of groups like that," I told him.

"I understand." He leaned down to put his hands on my shoulders and his pale dreads fell forward. "But they all came here for you. How about if you come out and just try to answer a few questions, then you can leave and I'll take care of the scheduling."

"But what do I say?"

"Just answer what they ask. I'll help you if you're not sure of something."

"Why are there so many?" I asked, peeking back out at the crowd.

"Word of mouth. You've healed enough people to get them talking. They're coming in and asking for the Hollywood Healer." His pale lips smiled. "I thought the name was great."

I didn't care so much about the name. "How am I gonna be able to see all those people?"

"Don't worry, Carson. They will just have to be patient. I won't let you get overworked. You see them as you can, and those who aren't willing to wait won't get to see you. Okay?"

"Okay," I said.

"Now let's go back out there, and I'll help you with the questions. Let's just give them a chance to see you."

I went back out, my hands getting all sweaty and my heart speeding up, as I answered questions. Casper took over when I didn't know what to say. He made me stay about ten minutes and then let me leave.

It was a business for Casper, and he was making money off of our whole arrangement, but he was helping me out, too. Not only would this job pay for my trip to Washington DC, but what other adult would have been willing to buy me the ticket? He believed that I was going to see my dad and never questioned me flying there alone. I knew I had to go along with Casper's business advice, even if that did mean talking in front of a big group, so that I could get to my dad. But the deeper reason I kept on working at the head shop was because of the feeling I got when I healed. I began to crave the feeling the way an athlete might feel compelled to play his sport, or a musician might yearn to pick up his guitar. I needed to heal. It was in my blood—part of who I was. I knew this was what I had to do.

Casper went back to scheduling appointments while I went out the back door and skated through the alley and away from the shop. The freedom of skating alone on the streets was a great feeling after the pressure of standing before that crowd.

It was a Monday. I knew exactly what I wanted to do with my free day. I took out the note that I'd kept in my pocket for over a week. She would be babysitting until five.

714 West Cherry was a tiny house at the front of an apartment complex. It had a small yard surrounded by a half-fallen fence. There was a big

plastic playhouse and toys all over a dirt area that looked like it had once been a lawn.

"Carson Calley," I heard from the screen door just before Rose pushed it open and walked out holding a baby in a diaper. "You actually showed up."

"Hey, Rose," I said, more nervous speaking to this one girl than I'd felt to the entire crowd at the head shop. I went in the gate and met her at the door. She had on short shorts and no shoes. The way the baby was holding onto her tank top, I could see one side of her black bra.

"Come inside," she said.

It was small and messy inside. Rose set the baby in a swing and buckled him in. The baby cried and cried as she tried sticking a pacifier in his mouth.

"I hate how much this kid screams," she said. "It's hard enough with him alone, but when his sister comes home from school and I have to deal with her too, I feel like I could pull my hair out."

"What's wrong with him?" I asked sitting on the carpet beside her.

"His mom says he has colic, whatever that is."

"What do you do for it?"

She threw her hands up. "You sit here and listen to him scream."

"Can I try something?" I asked.

"You can try anything you want," she said. "But nothing works. I've tried it all."

"It may seem kind of weird," I said through the crying. "But I'm a healer."

She started laughing. "You are weird, Carson," she said, getting up from the floor. "But I'll let you try your weird stuff on him so I can go finish the dishes."

The sound of dishes was the background noise as I held my hands over the baby and chanted, "*E ho mai.*" It was hard to completely lose myself in the moment as I was slightly self-conscious over Rose being there. I tried to tune her out but I couldn't. I fought through the distraction and I found just enough focus to gather the stars in my hands. They came slowly, but they came. And the healing began.

When the baby stopped crying Rose came back from the kitchen and sat on the floor beside me. "What'd you do?" She had a strange look on her face as she watched the calm baby in the swing.

"I healed him."

"You're freaking me out, Carson. Seriously, what did you do to him?"

"I," I shrugged. "I have this thing I can do with my hands. I don't know how I got it, but I can really heal people."

She just sat and watched the baby for a while, looking at me every now and then with squinting eyes. I was afraid she was going to laugh at me again, or say something mean, but instead she did something completely unexpected. She gave me a little smile and then pulled me up to the couch with her.

"I can't believe you shut him up," she said, coming close to me. "You deserve a reward." She put her lips to mine. They felt so good, I didn't want her to take them away. I closed my eyes as she pressed harder against me. Her taste, her smell, her touch—it was almost too much. My heart was pounding so hard, I was afraid she'd hear it.

When she pulled away, I licked my lips and caught my breath. "You taste like bubblegum," I said.

"It's bubblegum lip balm."

"Lip bomb?" I'd never heard of such a thing.

She laughed and hit me gently with the back of her hand. "*Balm,* not bomb."

"Whatever. I like it." She leaned in and kissed me again. This time she gave me her lips along with her tongue and we kissed for a while. I'd never felt anything like it. It was like the otherworldly feeling of a dream, but with all the sensations of being awake. She even put my hand over her bra and I held it there for as long as she'd let me. That was probably the best part—after all the time I'd spent staring at them, I finally had one in my hand.

Just when I thought it was getting good, she suddenly pulled away. "Did Faris say anything more about my tattoo yet?"

It took a second to switch modes and register her question. "Not yet," I answered and then tried to get close to her again.

She pushed me away. "I'm like done now." I wasn't, but I tried to be. "You said you could get me a tattoo and I'm still waiting. You don't just make promises to a girl if you can't keep them."

"I know," I said, looking down at the ground and trying not to think about the bubblegum taste still on my lips.

"I'm gonna be over by Faris' place on Friday. My great-aunt has another protest rally she needs me at." She rolled her eyes.

"Your great-aunt?" I asked. "The one in the wheelchair?"

"Yeah, she's crazy, but my dad makes me go with her." She got up from the couch and started cleaning up the toys all over the carpet. "The rally should end by three. And once my great-aunt leaves, I'll come over to the shop. And I expect you to have it all worked out by then."

"The thing is—" I couldn't avoid the truth any longer. "Faris says he won't do it. Says you're too young." She turned back to me with a mean face. "But I'm making a lot of money with this new job I got. So if you could find another artist who'll do it, I'll pay for it. I swear, no matter how much it costs, I'll pay for it."

"How am I gonna find someone who'll do it?" She glared at me. "No one will give me one unless it's a favor. And I was counting on you, Carson." She started doing that thing again with her eyes, squeezing them shut over and over. "Just leave," she said throwing her hands over her face. "Seriously. Get out of here, Carson. I don't want to see you anymore."

I got up from the couch and tried to get close to her again. "I'm sorry, Rose."

"Leave!" This time she screamed so loud, it got the baby crying again.

I took my skateboard and left. Skating through the streets on my way home, I practiced over and over in my head the things I might say to convince Faris to give her a tattoo. There had to be a way to make him do it.

I couldn't get Rose off my mind all day. I kept tasting the bubblegum from the bomb she left on my lips.

Twenty-eight

"You gotta do this for me, Faris," I pleaded with him in his station as he cleaned up the tattoo machine from his last customer. "I know you said no way before, but I swear, we need to work something out. I'll pay for it. I mean, I'll pay double for it. Things are different between me and Rose now, and I don't want to blow it. Please say you'll give her just one little tattoo."

Faris didn't say a word. He just went on cleaning up.

"She's the one in here last week, right?" Beans called from his station. "The one who came in and looked through my book while she waited for you?"

"Yeah," I said.

"Did she tell you what kind of tattoo she's looking to get?"

"No."

"Mijo," he shook his head. "You got to know a girl's *intention* before you bust your balls trying to do her a *favor.*"

"Please, Beans," I pleaded, walking over to him. "I'll pay you double what it costs."

He shook his head again, sticking his tongue out and clicking the tongue ring on his teeth.

"Triple," I said. "I'll pay you triple."

"Think about this," he tried reasoning with me. "You give the girl what she wants, then she takes it and leaves you. But if you hold out and don't give it right away, she'll stick around hoping for it. No?" He arched his eyebrows, taking all the silver up with them.

I thought about it. "No," I shook my head. "You don't know this girl. I just gotta do this for her." I spoke softer so just he would hear. "I kissed her."

"Yeah?" He smiled. "Your first?" I nodded. "How 'bout this," he said folding his arms. "I'll give you a tattoo, in honor of your first kiss. Then it's for you to keep even if she bails."

A throaty laugh came from across the room. We both looked over to Faris. "If you give him a tattoo every time he falls for a girl," Faris said, "he'll look like me by the time he's eighteen."

"No, just this one time," Beans said. "It's got special meaning."

Faris looked over at Beans.

"Come on, Faris," Beans said. "It was his first kiss."

"Just this one," Faris eventually agreed. "But no way that girl's getting one. End of story."

I knew Faris probably wouldn't change his mind, but after that kiss, I had to give it one last shot. I would've done anything to kiss her again. And there was no way she would if I didn't get her a tattoo. It felt like the end of a bad movie, where you walk out of the theater really sad because it shouldn't have ended that way. And just like with a movie, I had no control to go back and fix the story.

There was nothing left to do but take Beans up on his offer. I'd get a tattoo myself and then just avoid House of Freaks on Friday so I wouldn't have to see Rose and tell her no. Faris and Beans would cover for me.

The next day, I went to the shop with an idea for my new tattoo. I knew exactly how I wanted to remember Rose and that first kiss she gave me on West Cherry. Beans sketched my idea on paper and he got it just right. It didn't take long. I had it done on the other shoulder, opposite my black crow.

"That's one I've never seen," Faris remarked as he and Beans stood back, admiring the art. "Clever." He nodded. "It's clever."

"It's genius," Beans argued.

Holding my shoulder toward the mirror I looked at the new image on my skin. It was perfect, the red lips with a black fuse, lit and preparing to blow up. I would always remember my first taste of a woman, and the explosive feelings it brought on, when I looked at the tattoo—my lip bomb.

Twenty-nine

It was a Sunday morning when I met with Lolo for what would be the last time. In this final session, she told me that her work with me was done. I didn't understand how only a handful of sessions could teach me enough about healing, but she explained that, ultimately, healing was not something that could be taught. Lolo made it clear that I already had the gift. She couldn't add to that.

"But it feels like we just got started."

"You don't need me, Carson," she said, her native accent completely gone. "You never really did."

"But what if I have questions?"

"You already have all the answers inside of you," she said, pulling a pack of gum out of her purse. "Don't doubt yourself, Carson. You're an amazing kid." She held out a stick of gum. "Want one?"

It wasn't the kind of gift I was hoping my great mentor would leave me with, but I took it anyway. "Is there a way I could get a hold of you if I really need to ask you something about healing?"

She stared at me for moment with uncertainty. "I don't think that's a good idea."

"Please?" I laced my fingers together and held my hands up. "Please, Lolo? I don't have anyone else to ask."

She reached into her purse and pulled out a card. "Okay, I'll give you my agent's card. Only if you really, really need me, you call her, and then she knows how to get a hold of me."

I took the card.

"I want you to know I am honored that I got to spend time with you," she said putting her arms out and pulling me into a firm embrace. My arms rested lightly around her.

"*E ho mai,*" she began to chant softly as she held me. I wasn't in the mood to sing along and just stood there until she finished.

"I have to go now, Carson." She gave me a kiss on my cheek. "You will do great things in your life."

✻ ✻ ✻

Some people have a childhood home they go back to when they need comfort—a place with family and history. The closest thing to that for me was House of Freaks. When I got there, I found a sign on the door that read: "We'll be back at 12:00." It was just about that time. I took a seat on the crate by myself, watching a bunch of crows land in the street in front of me. It reminded me of Faris' story about the girl who thought crows were angels that showed up to help her get through dark times. Now that I'd just lost Lolo, maybe they'd come to comfort me.

Faris came walking up, holding a bag.

"Carson," he grinned. I liked that he was always happy to see me.

"Hey, Faris."

"I got a roast beef sandwich here," he said, taking a seat on the stool and opening up the bag. "It's big enough for two." He pulled out half the sandwich and handed it to me.

"Thanks," I said.

"You okay?" he asked with a mouthful.

I shrugged, chewing my food. "Yeah," I said. "Just needed somewhere to go."

"Glad you came here." He looked my way, giving me a little nod, and then got back to his sandwich.

We ate our lunch watching people walk by on the sidewalk. A couple tourists came up to us at one point and asked if they could take a picture with Faris. He always said yes when that happened.

When Faris' next customer showed up, I didn't want to leave yet. I went inside and looked through magazines while Faris worked. Listening in on their conversation, I was thinking about how Faris had a way with people. He was one of the best listeners I'd ever known. He seemed like the kind of guy who'd probably done it all, so people felt safe telling him stuff.

They would tell him things they couldn't tell anyone else.

It made me think about the old church days with my mom. People went there to find inspiration and work through problems, but it wasn't always the safest place to do that. They were pretty clean-cut and proper there and had a lot of strict rules. They wouldn't have been too comfortable with the kinds of people I'd seen with Faris. I got to thinking that House of Freaks was more than just a place to get a tattoo. With Faris running the shop, in some ways it was like a church for those who wouldn't fit into a regular one.

When Faris was almost finished with the tattoo, he asked me to go in the back and get him a towel. I dropped the magazine back onto the table and went to get the towel for him.

"Whata you think?" Faris asked me, motioning toward the guy's arm. Centered between his shoulder and elbow was a portrait of an old guy with serious eyes and a long beard. Leaning against the mirror was a black and white print of the same guy. It was an amazing match.

"That's good," I said, blown away by Faris' talent. "It's exactly like the picture."

Faris stepped back admiring his art. There was barely a smile on his lips, but I could see it in his eyes.

"Is this your grandfather?" I asked the guy.

"No." It was a laugh. "It's Herman Melville. Wrote *Moby Dick?*"

I nodded. I knew the book. "Why'd you want that?" I was curious.

"Inspiration." He shrugged.

"Justin's a writer," Faris explained.

"A writer. That's cool," I said, eyeing the guy, who looked more like a skater.

"You read much?" he asked me.

"Yeah," I said, thinking about how my mom hadn't brought me books in quite a while. "I like reading."

"Here," he said, reaching down into his backpack on the floor and pulling out a book. He took a pen, quickly scribbled something inside and then tossed it to me. It was a novel. I turned it over and his picture was on the back flap.

"Thanks," I said, smiling. A real author. It was another cool moment at the shop, meeting a kind of celebrity. It was right up there with the time I met the drummer of a punk band, a pro-surfer, and of course Pepper, the Playboy bunny.

I was feeling a lot better by the time I left the shop. Things always felt better after hanging out with Faris. But it didn't last for long.

Late that night, in a conversation with my mom, I found out that Lolo had ended up getting a part in a movie and that's why she couldn't see me anymore. She was to play the role of an Indonesian healer in a feature film. My mom seemed to find it funny that Lolo the healer would be paid to pretend she was a healer. My mom laughed and laughed in her drunken state, saying her time with me made her good enough to make it to the big screen. I didn't find it funny at all.

Thirty

It was the job that gave me enough money all at once to get my ticket to Washington DC. Veronica Sterling, an Oscar-winning actress, had her manager call Casper to request a session with me. She offered to pay a thousand dollars.

Veronica had been diagnosed with breast cancer and wasn't responding to the chemo. Looking for a miracle, she'd made arrangements to fly to the small town of Lourdes, France, so she could take a bath in the holy water at a sacred grotto blessed by the Virgin Mary. But then she heard about me and changed her plans. I asked Casper how she'd heard about me and he just said my name was all over town.

She came to the head shop late so that fans wouldn't see her and complicate our session. Her driver brought her to the back alley under the glowing light of a full moon. I'd been given explicit instructions not to chat with her. She just wanted to be healed.

I was inside the shop watching through the opened door when she arrived. I saw Casper hold his hand out to her as she stepped from the back seat of the limo. She wore a loose-fitting gray dress and a pink crocheted beanie over her head. Most of her hair was gone from the chemo. She wore no makeup on her face, but she was beautiful anyway. You could tell she had been born to be a star.

Veronica lifted her eyes to the sky, staring at the full moon for a moment, and then she entered the shop. Seeing me there, she halted. She narrowed her eyes as she looked me over. "You're the healer?" I nodded. She looked back at Casper who also confirmed with a nod. She looked up at the ceiling and around the place. "Is this a joke? Am I being Punk'd?"

"He is young," Casper said in that confident voice of his, "but the gift is purer with youth."

She turned back to me and looked me over. With a shake of her head and a surrendered toss of her hands, she smiled. "Heal me if you can."

I tried to keep my expression neutral, but I just had to smile back. A woman this powerful was giving me a chance. "Follow me," I said quietly, motioning to the back room.

"Wait. Can we have the session outside, under the moon?" she whispered. "My driver can keep an eye out if anyone comes." I nodded, liking her idea. She took my hand and I followed her out to the back alley.

She went to the limo, briefly spoke to her driver, and returned with a bulky white fur coat. She tossed it on the ground in a small open space between the trash cans and the back door and sat down on it with her legs folded.

"Faux fur." She smirked, and then reached for my hand, pulling me down to join her.

Sitting beside her in the alley, on soft, white fur, with the back of the building, the trash cans, and a black limo as our surroundings, I began the chant. "*E ho mai,*" I sang softly, closing my eyes. But then I opened them again. I didn't want to close myself off from this moment. There was something oddly spectacular about sitting in an alley with a famous actress under a glowing full moon. I wanted to witness it with my eyes and hold it in my memory.

We sat facing each other, holding hands, looking into each other, and creating what felt like an exchange of energy. The *mauiamu* came easily. We were perfectly synced—my giving and her accepting—nothing awkward or foreign-feeling to taint our perfect connection. I could feel that I was healing her, but it went even further than that. She was giving something to me. It's hard to hold hands with a woman like Veronica Sterling and not feel her greatness. She was one of those people born with a little extra light shining through. Being open and receptive to her light—even a little hungry for it—I felt a bit like the full moon above us. She was the sun, and I could feel myself reflecting her. I could tell this moment had the potential to alter my life. And I had no doubt that it would change hers.

After what seemed like hours, I stood up, confident that Veronica Sterling had been cured. She gave me a hug and went inside the limo. Her driver shut the door and briefly went over to see Casper, then got behind the wheel. I watched as they drove away and disappeared around the corner. Casper went back into the shop, but I stayed there in the alley for quite some time alone. I had to ease my way back to reality. You don't hang with the stars and then drop back down to the ground within seconds. It's a slow descent.

I sat against the stucco wall, tapping the old, rusty metal trash can beside me to re-awaken my senses. The tips of my fingers felt the cold, rough metal, and my ears took in the dull, rhythmic sounds. It started softly, slowly. Tap, tap, tap, tap. The sound seemed to feed something inside of me. I stayed with it, closing my eyes, and soon the tapping progressed from tips of fingers to full hands. My hands hit the sides of the can over and over with a rhythm I didn't even know I had in me. The rapid tinny sounds echoed through the alley and I was taken back—two thousands years before—to a time when my destiny was stolen from me. I began drumming even faster. I wouldn't let my destiny be stolen from me in this life. I would stay my course and make sure fate gave back what it owed me. I would become the great healer of our time—a healer so great, he could bring back the dead. The drum spoke to me in my old native tongue and I could feel the connection between the two lives. My breathing grew heavier and my skin glistened with moisture that made it feel like the light breeze was biting me. I was back from the stars, completely grounded and alive.

"Shut the hell up!" came a shout from the other end of the alley. I suddenly stopped, breathless and wet. I looked around for the person behind the voice, but he chose not to show himself. I got up from behind the trash cans. It wasn't quite the ending I'd anticipated for this spiritually charged night, but it did the job. Quietly, I stepped back inside the head shop and closed the door behind me.

Thirty-one

Summer ended and school was back in. The very first day, Rose saw me and went off on me. She came up to my locker and yelled at me for being a liar and a loser. She kept yelling, not giving me a chance to talk, and ended up blinking her eyes like crazy until she threw her hands over her face and rushed off. Every time I saw her that week, she had something mean to say. I didn't say anything back. I just hoped she would get over it soon so I wouldn't walk around school scared of running into her.

It was a bad week, but Friday after school, something happened to make me start feeling better. I went to the head shop and Casper told me he'd bought my ticket to Washington DC. I held the airline confirmation ticket and stared at the date only three weeks away. After my night with Veronica Sterling I was ready to try it. The intensity I had felt with her told me that I just might be capable of going deep enough to resurrect my dad. But even if depth wasn't enough, even if Lolo was right that the dead couldn't come back, I wouldn't be completely disappointed with my trip. I couldn't wait to just finally be with my dad. He was a hero. He deserved a visit from his son.

My mom was gone again when I got back from the head shop. I tucked my confirmation ticket in my drawer, under my T-shirts. I microwaved a frozen pizza for dinner, and then I took my skateboard out to the streets.

I went to the Fonda and met up with Buddy and the guys. I got there just as they decided the tip jar was full enough. We went to buy their weed, and then skated to a party. I didn't usually go inside the parties that the older guys took us to. They were mostly for high school kids, so I skated outside with the younger guys while we waited. But this party, Buddy told me, was at an eighth graders' place. I was old enough to go in.

I recognized a few people from school but they didn't seem to know who I was. The first person who did recognize me was Rose. I had no idea she would be there. She saw me and headed straight for me. "It's the loser," she said, holding up her red plastic cup as she approached me. "The loser with the bird tattoo," she said, pulling up my sleeve—but she pulled up the wrong side. Instead of a black crow, she was looking at my lip bomb. She put her hand on her hip. "He wouldn't give me one but he gave you another one?"

I shrugged, embarrassed that she was looking at the tattoo I got because of our kiss.

"What is this?" she held my arm and leaned in to look at it. "Lips?"

"It's a lip bomb." She didn't seem to understand, so I explained, "You know, from that day you were babysitting, and your bubblegum—"

"What are you talking about? Lip balm?" She skewed her eyes. "Wait, are you saying bomb again?"

"Yeah." I threw my hands up, frustrated that she could manage to make me feel small no matter what I did.

"Are you serious?" She threw her head back in a fit of laughter. "Oh my God, you are so lame. You tattooed a lip *bomb*?" She folded over, holding her stomach as she laughed, spilling her beer all over my shoes. She called a few of her friends over and told them the story while I just stood there, the butt of her joke. I even lifted my sleeve for everyone to see how stupid I was. The laughter hurt. My embarrassment was too great to do anything but pretend to laugh along.

"Is this the guy that was gonna get you the tattoo with Billy's name?" one of her friends asked.

"He said he would, but he totally flaked."

"Who's Billy?" I asked.

"My boyfriend," Rose said.

"You have a boyfriend?"

"He's still away. He's in juvie and won't be back home for another year. I wanted to surprise him with a tattoo," she said, trying to be cute. "But," she lifted her chin and that pissed-off look that came so natural was back on her face, "looks like you're not gonna be the one to help me get it."

She walked away with her friends and left me standing there alone. I felt embarrassed just standing there, but when I looked around, I realized no one even noticed me. I made my way to the door, practically invisible.

I didn't tell any of the guys I was leaving. I left the party on my own and skated down the street. The rush of the night's air in my face wasn't enough to cool off the fire that began growing inside me. I kept recalling the way Rose had laughed at me and how she'd made a fool of me. I heard her call me loser over and over in my mind, and worst of all, I thought about her wanting a tattoo with her *boyfriend's* name. She had a boyfriend. She had been using me. It was all too much.

I stopped there on La Cienega and walked over to a row of shops. I thrust my fist at a wooden door over and over but couldn't punch through it. I wrapped my bloodied knuckles and fingers with my good hand as I crouched down in pain. I held it for a little while, contemplating a better release. That's when I picked myself back up, and without hesitating, took my skateboard and swung it like a baseball bat against the front window of a barbershop. With each swing I went harder and harder. Eventually the glass shattered. I ran to the next window, and after only three swings, I broke through the glass again, but this time an alarm sounded. Wide-eyed and alert, I ran from the sidewalk and out to the street.

I skated in a mad rush back toward our motel. When I heard the police sirens coming my way, I turned down a side street. There, in front of an apartment, was an overgrown bush. I took my skateboard and hid behind it. The bush shook with my movements as I adjusted myself between it and the stucco wall.

"Hey!" I heard from a window above me. "Hey!" The shout grew louder. "Who's down there?" I kept as still as I could, but then lost grip of my skateboard. It fell and landed in the dirt upside down. I went to grab it, but my hand just grazed the wheels there in the dark. The wheels began to spin, making a low whir—and giving away my hiding place. I ran out from the bush and into the street. I didn't stop, skating hard through the dark streets. Every time a car light came up behind me I was sure it was a cop. My nerves were on edge, so I kept up the pace until I made it back home.

Lying in bed that night, I couldn't fall asleep. Why couldn't I control myself when my anger built up? My hands were so good at healing people, but why was I also compelled to use them to destroy things? If people knew about this side of me, they would never trust me to heal them. And if I ever got caught, I'd go to jail. My hand found its way to the black crow on my arm and gave a gentle squeeze. I was pretty sure my dad was watching over me the times I lost my temper, and that was why I'd never been caught. I knew I needed to hold it together at least long enough to get to Washington DC. I hung onto the slight hope that my dad might come back to teach me how to control my anger and be the great man I was supposed to be.

Thirty-two

When I got home from school, the clerk up front in our motel stopped me. He told me that my mom had been taken away in an ambulance, and he told me which hospital she went to. I rushed out of there and took a taxi to the hospital.

"I'm here to see," I hesitated with her name. I'd never gotten used to saying it. The receptionist watched me with an expectant look. She needed a name. "Juliette Bravo. She's my mom."

Without any reaction to the name, the receptionist looked it up in the computer and gave me a room number.

"What's wrong with her?" I asked before heading to the room.

"Let me get a doctor to help you," she answered and paged someone.

I remembered the day my mom changed her name. I was seven. We took a bus to downtown LA where all the tall buildings are. The streets were alive with car horns chattering, and strangers on the sidewalks rushing along. My mom held my hand with a firm grip as we walked. The flow of hurried people generated a collective tempo, and we couldn't help but get caught up in it. Despite her high-heeled shoes, and my young legs, my mom and I kept the pace. When we finally reached the address she was looking for, we stepped out of the great pedestrian wave and slipped through a revolving door into one of the buildings.

My mom still held my hand in the elevator, but let go once we reached the office on the ninth floor. She needed her hands to run her fingers through her long hair, to wipe at the skin under her eyes, to smooth down her shirt, and to adjust her necklace. I didn't see what difference it made, but she seemed satisfied, and then took my hand again. She held it the entire time we waited in the long line. She made small talk with the people around us. My mom was good at talking with strangers.

"Maggie Calley," she identified herself to the man behind the counter when we finally made it to the front of the line. While the man typed into his computer, she looked down at me and smiled.

"New name?" the man asked.

"Juliette Bravo."

At the age of seven I didn't like the idea of my mom suddenly changing her name, especially since it was different from mine. I liked who she was. I didn't want her to become someone new. The man behind the counter printed out a couple papers and handed them to my mom with a clipboard. We walked back to the seating area where she was to fill them out.

"But, Mom, I like your name."

"It's just not me anymore," she said, turning toward me as we walked. "Maggie is a—" her eyes searched upward for the right word "—a simple, ordinary, *nice* name." She cringed.

"Well, you're nice."

She gave me a smile, tucked the clipboard under her arm, and pulled me toward her. "Oh, Carson." She smoothed my hair with her long fingers. "How do I explain this? Let's just say Maggie doesn't fit me anymore. I've grown out of it."

I was confused.

"Remember those orange sneakers you used to love?" she went on, motioning to a couple of plastic chairs. I sat down. She stood before me as she explained. "And then they started getting tight? And finally your feet wouldn't fit in them anymore?"

I nodded.

"Well, it's like that. The name Maggie is too tight on me. It's squeezing me," she said, tightening her arms and fists up to her chest. "I need a bigger name."

"Juliette Bravo?" I repeated the name she was about to take.

"Yes," she beamed, and then adjusted her skirt again just before sitting down beside me. "Juliette Bravo. It's beautiful and bold and it fits me."

"Where'd you find that name?"

"I found it on an airplane," she said, setting the clipboard on her lap. "When Jackson took me on his friend's private plane."

"When I stayed with Molly that time?" Molly was an actress friend of my mom's. I remembered she had a cat. We didn't see her much anymore.

"Yeah, that time," she confirmed, looking down at the questionnaire and writing in answers. "Whenever the pilot had to identify our plane to ground control, he would say into the radio, 'This is N-2-something-something Juliette Bravo.' I fell in love with the name. Every time I heard him say it, I felt like he was talking to me."

"Does Jackson like your new name?"

She gave a mischievous smile. "Jackson thinks everything I do is a little crazy. But that's what makes me irresistible to him."

She went back to filling out her paperwork. "Ju-li-ette Bra-vo," she enunciated her new name as she penned her loopy signature at the bottom of the form. She brought the clipboard up to her chest with both arms over it, as if she were hugging it. "Today, February eleventh, I declare my new birthday. Happy Birthday to Juliette Bravo. We'll go get cake and candles on the way home."

I held my mom's hand as her high wooden heels clicked their way back to the man at the counter. After he looked over her paperwork and typed a few things in his computer, my mom's new name became official.

Back at the hospital, a woman in a white coat arrived a few minutes later. The receptionist told her who I was.

"Is your father here?" she asked.

"He died," I said.

"Oh, I'm sorry." She bowed her head. "Are you here with your grandparents? Or another adult?"

"No, but I'm almost fourteen." I thought I should tell her. Maybe she didn't realize I wasn't as young as I looked.

The doctor smiled at me. "Okay."

She told me how my mom had come in with abdominal pains, barely able to walk. She said something about her liver, and how too much drinking can damage it. My mom apparently had had this condition for quite some time. The doctor was vague when I asked how long it would take to heal. She just said it was serious. Then she asked me a bunch of questions about where we lived and other stuff. All I wanted to do was go to my mom. I rushed down the hall as soon as she was done.

I went into her room and found a pale, sickly woman with an IV in her arm, tubes up her nose, and the white hospital sheet covering her body. She looked nothing at all like my mom.

"Carson." Her voice was limp, and her lips were barely able to lift to a smile.

"Mom," I said, sitting on the hospital bed beside her. The other beds in her room were empty. The machines around her gave an occasional beep. "What happened?"

"Oh," she said, trying to sing the word, but it sounded groggy. "My heart is having a hard time."

I narrowed my eyes. "Your heart? They said that you have something wrong with your liver. From all the drinking."

"What do they know." She tried to laugh but the tubes in her nose made it hard for her. "It's my heart. You can't live with a broken heart as long as I have and expect the rest of my body to function."

"But, Mom." How could she get to that point and still not admit that she drank too much? "They said it's about your drinking."

"Don't believe them. They don't know me like I know me," she whispered, too tired to continue. She closed her eyes and fell asleep.

I didn't say anything. It wasn't worth fighting over. I just sat there and watched her breathe. Could she be dying? The idea frightened me. I knew what I needed to do.

I closed my eyes and began the *E ho mai* chant inside my mind. I tried taking myself as deep into my spiritual source as I could go so that I'd have the power to heal my mom. Then I began to chant it out loud, over and over, and soon felt compelled to lift my open palms over my mom's body. I held them above her and felt the tiny white stars rushing into her. As I summoned more stars, I felt pressure building and building through my arms, and then, in an intense rush, the *mauiamu* poured from my hands, drenching my mom with its light. It was as if she was glowing. I felt electric, on fire, the source of her radiance. I couldn't get myself to pull away.

Her body hungrily took in the tiny stars and I had to keep giving and giving. I couldn't tell how long the healing lasted—it could have been an hour, it could have been fifteen minutes. When I opened my eyes, I saw a man standing at the door watching us. Almost immediately, the intense spiritual connection was broken. My hands, still hot from the *mauiamu*, dropped to my sides and I impulsively coughed, catching my breath.

The man stood there for another few seconds, then he walked away. As he turned, I noticed his long, gray ponytail. It was Jackson.

I turned my attention back to my mom and touched her arm lightly. She opened her eyes. "Mom," I said, almost surprised. "How do you feel?"

Her eyes wandered upward as if considering what I'd said. When she looked back at me, she wore a defiant smile. "And they said I'd be stuck in this place for a week. Hell, I feel like a million bucks." She tried to laugh and the tubes in her nose gave the laugh a nasal sound.

I stared at her in amazement. The sickly stranger I'd walked in on was gone. My old mom was back. "I healed you while you slept."

She just stared at me with narrowed eyes. She placed her hand by her stomach and pressed down a few times. "It doesn't hurt anymore." Her head shook from side to side on the pillow and her eyes closed for a moment. When she opened them she said, "I don't know what I'd do without you."

"I've had a lot of practice lately." I wanted her to know. "Remember I told you about Casper's place? He set up a back room for me and I've healed a lot of people there."

"A back room at Casper's shop." She sat up and propped the pillow behind her. "It's like you're following in your mother's footsteps. I've got a back room at Nelson's place, you've got one at Casper's, and we're each giving Hollywood our own little brand of miracles." She winked. The way she was looking at me, it felt like she really saw me. Maybe it took a trip to the hospital to get her in a better place. I hoped things could start getting better now between us.

"I think Jackson was here," I said. "He was watching from the hall as I healed you, and then he left."

"Jackson?" She pulled away from her pillow and leaned forward. "He was here?"

"Yeah, I saw him outside the room then he left."

"You probably scared him off." She started running her fingers through her hair and wiping at her eyes. "I must look like hell. I don't want Jackson seeing me like this. Carson, would you mind running to the drugstore and picking up a little lipstick for me?" She licked her lips. "And a little blush? And, maybe some gum?" She told me to jot down the kinds she wanted on the little pad next to the bed.

I left her hospital room holding a torn piece of paper with the words mystical penny, copper sunset, and spearmint—lipstick, blush and gum. Once I mentioned Jackson, she didn't even care that I was there anymore—except for the fact that I could run to the store for her. I hated being second to him, yet again.

I felt the anger coming on and it was the middle of the day. I couldn't get away with doing something destructive in the daylight but I wanted to release some of the feelings inside. I found myself starting to run—pounding my feet to the concrete. I ran harder and harder, faster and faster. My feet pounding and my heart rapidly beating felt kind of good. I ran and ran down the sidewalk, weaving my way through scattered pedestrians. When I got to the drugstore five blocks from the hospital, I couldn't stop. I had to keep going to relieve the feelings inside. There were no clear thoughts going through my mind, I was just my forward-moving legs, my fisted hands, my pumping arms, my panting breath, and my sweaty skin. I ran the entire five miles back to the motel. By the time I got there, I was too exhausted to feel any more of the anger.

Once in our room, I threw the torn piece of paper with the words mystical penny, copper sunset, and spearmint into the trash. Then I stripped off my wet clothes and took a shower. Too tired to think about my day or even worry about my mom waiting for me to come back, I passed out on the twin bed, right on top of the bedspread.

Thirty-three

"So you think you healed her, huh?" Faris had his arms folded over his chest. I'd studied the designs and characters on his arms so many times, they'd become as familiar as his face. At the moment my eyes were stuck on the crimson cross that covered his biceps.

"I *know* I healed her." My hands gripped the edge of the crate where I sat. "I mean, when I got there she looked like she was dying, and after I worked on her, she was fine—totally fine."

"What'd the doctors say?"

I shrugged. "She didn't tell me what they said, but she's back home now."

She came back the next day and never even asked why I didn't get her stuff from the drugstore. She was back to being distracted. Jackson had given her a ride from the hospital and was waiting out front for her. She didn't say much before leaving with him again.

"Your mom's a lucky lady to have a kid who could zap away her pain." His grin suggested he doubted my story.

"And I'm a lucky guy to have a friend that doesn't even believe me," I said, getting up from the crate.

"Hey, hey," Faris' tone was almost apologetic. "Don't go getting pissed off at me just 'cause I don't know anything about this healing thing you do."

"But I told you about it so many times." I stood there facing him. "I told you what I do and what happens when I do it."

"Yeah." He wrinkled up his eyes, the lines going deeper than usual. "I know what you told me. It's just—" he reached for the extra cigarette he kept behind his ear. "I just think that if you're looking hard enough for something, you're gonna get yourself to see it. You know what I mean?"

"Yeah, I know exactly what you mean. You don't believe in my power."

"Ah, Carson, sit back down. I think we need to talk." His voice was firm this time, like the way a dad might sound. Reluctantly, I sat back down.

"You're not a little kid anymore." He looked directly at me as he spoke instead of looking out at the street. "I know thirteen isn't quite an adult, but you've had to grow up a lot faster than most kids your age. I think I need to talk with you more like an adult now." I didn't answer—I just stared back at him. "I've known you now for a couple of years. You're a bright kid, a really bright kid, and I told you plenty of times that I expect great things from you. But those great things won't come if you don't eventually pull yourself out of that fantasy land your mom created for you."

"What?" I was pissed.

"Hear me out. Your mom gave you a lot of great stories to get you through your childhood, and she did the right thing. She did. Stories like that give kids hope, they keep them optimistic. Look at Santa Claus—he taught kids all over the world that if you're good, you'll get good stuff coming your way. But here's the thing, eventually you gotta learn that there really is no Santa. He was just a tool. You don't wanna be waiting by the fireplace at twenty-one wondering where the hell your presents are."

It felt like his words just hit me in the stomach. He'd listened to me over the years and always had an agreeable response. Now he was telling me he hadn't even believed me. "Look, Faris." I got up from the crate, my hands clenched in fists. "You don't even know about what my mom told me. I mean, maybe sometimes she exaggerated her stuff when she was drinking." My voice shot up a couple pitches. "Or she made some parts up because she couldn't remember everything, but my mom didn't lie to me."

I had doubts about some of the things my mom had said over the years, but there was no denying the truth over her claim that I was a healer. It was happening before my eyes—as well as the eyes of all those strangers I'd already healed. I couldn't explain how she knew, but she knew. And for just this one bit of truth that I was certain of, I felt compelled to defend my mom's honor. And it felt good, sort of like old times, being on her side again.

"I'm not saying she lied."

"If you actually saw what my hands can do, you'd know that she told me the truth about me being a healer."

Faris threw his hands up as if surrendering. "It's your life, man. All I'm saying is that you got to get straight with yourself. Don't buy into anyone's ideas about who you are and what you need to do."

I didn't have anything else to say to him. Without a word, I just walked away.

Thirty-four

After her trip to the hospital, my mom had one more really bad night and ended up in rehab. She was admitted for forty-five days and wasn't allowed contact with the outside. I found out about it from a friend of hers, Winnie. She was the one who'd gone drinking with my mom the night before, and was there the next morning when my mom agreed to let Jackson take her to rehab. I didn't know Winnie; I just met her when she came to the motel to tell me. She had promised my mom she would let me know what had happened, and then would watch after me while my mom was gone. She followed through on the first part, but not the second. I was okay with her never coming back, though. I knew I could take care of myself.

I made enough money to get my own food and I was able to pay for the motel on my own. I took cash to the front desk each week, telling them my mom sent me down to pay. No one questioned it. And since Winnie was technically responsible for me, no one came to check on me.

It was my birthday. I was fourteen years old. It was the first birthday that I didn't see my mom. Buddy said he and the guys had something special planned. I was glad it wasn't going to be totally ignored.

We met behind the dumpster at six o'clock. It was still light out. About five of our friends were standing in a circle, hiding a surprise for me in the center. Buddy kept me away from the circle until the guys were ready to reveal it.

I waited by a curb, watching a gathering of crows up on the wires. They seemed to be scoping out a couple of leftover fast-food bags that had been tossed into the lot near the dumpster. Every now and then, one of the birds would swoop down toward the bags, but then cautiously rush back to the wire, not yet brave enough to get close to us.

"Okay, bring him over here," someone called out and Buddy led me to the circle. As I approached, they opened up to reveal a big aluminum tray of brownies with birthday candles stuck in them. One of the guys said he had his sister bake them for me. I smiled. My mom had never made me birthday cake, or cookies, or brownies.

"Okay, okay," Buddy announced, pushing guys aside to make his way to the brownies, "time to light up the candles." He reached in his pocket and pulled out a lighter. "Let's light up, boys," he called out.

The circle was close, guys pushing each other and bumping up against each other as they sang a deep, tuneless version of the birthday song. Just as they finished, I blew out the candles. They cheered and grunted as everyone grabbed at the brownies. We devoured them like animals. I was so caught up in the frenzy of my birthday celebration that I didn't realize how many I had eaten. In a short time, I was feeling lightheaded. We stayed there clumped together even after the tray was empty. There was a lot of wrestling and hitting and smack-talking and laughing. It was fun for a while until my mind and vision grew foggy and my movements slowed to half speed. It was still light outside as I broke from the group, stumbled away from the dumpster, and collapsed against a wall nearby.

I vaguely remember looking up to see Buddy pull it out from his backpack, my eyes drawn to what looked like a yellow wishbone. He was saying something about giving me one more present. "I know how much you like crows," he said, grabbing my arm near my tattoo. His grip was strong. I struggled to stand up, but he pushed me back down. It made my drowsy eyes momentarily go wide. That's when I clearly saw it was a slingshot in his hand.

Buddy pointed to the gathering of crows that had finally made their way down to the fast-food bags in the parking lot. I watched him hold the slingshot up to his eye, pull back on the rubber band, hold the position, then let go.

The crows took off in a swarm. I watched the flying shadows against the dimming sky. The next thing I saw was Buddy, standing over me, smiling. He held a large black crow by its wing and dropped it in my lap. The weight of the bird jolted me. It was heavier than I expected. "Happy birthday, man. I got it in one shot."

Dazed, I looked down. The wounded bird released a weak sound as it tried to lift its bloody wing. I was startled, instinctually pushing it off my lap. It rolled and stumbled there on the pavement and then fell to its side. I leaned down to see if it was still alive. Its eyes were blinking, but they didn't close from top to bottom, they closed from the sides. I moved closer, my face just inches from the crow, fascinated. Blink, blink, blink. I shook my head, trying to clear some of the fog inside so I could figure out what to do.

The rest of the guys ran over. Seeing the wounded crow, they decided to go crow hunting with Buddy's yellow slingshot, leaving me alone with the first victim.

I'd always been so thrilled to tell the tale of my father killing a crow, and yet sitting there with my own wounded crow made me uneasy. With just a touch of clarity hitting my brain, I knew I needed to heal this crow. I lifted my hands and set them over the bird as I knelt beside it. *"E ho mai,"* I chanted, slurring it more than singing it. Trying to gather the strength to heal, I barely had the balance to sit up and touch the shivering bird. I tried to imagine the stars, the *mauiamu.* They twinkled in my mind, like glitter, but they had no power. They just aimlessly twinkled and danced along, not allowing me to take hold of them.

A weak cry came from the crow. And another. And another. It was begging me to help it, but I couldn't. Whatever they had put in the brownies made me too weak to conjure up the strength I needed to heal the dying crow. I gathered the broken black bird in my arms and tried to stand up. I fell once, but managed to get to my feet, still holding the crow. I stumbled away from the group.

"Hey, man, where are you going?" Buddy called out. "What, are you on something?" That got a big laugh.

I began running, slowly at first, then faster. I ran out of the parking lot and to the front of the Fonda Theater, and then down Hollywood Boulevard. I didn't have a destination, I only felt like I needed to run. People on the sidewalks jumped out of my way, cringing at the sight of me running with a crow in my hands, its blood on my T-shirt. When I started losing my breath, I slowed to a fast walk. I noticed more and more disgusted faces looking my way, yet they didn't seem real. It was dreamlike, hazy, other-worldly. The only thing that was real was the bird in my arms.

I turned down a side street, wanting to get away from the nightmarish crowd, and that's when I saw him. A man in a long black coat. His face was pale and he had black lines drawn around his eyes. He was standing in the alley behind a liquor store. He stepped out to reveal himself just as I was passing. It was as if he knew I was coming.

"What do you have there?" A little spittle escaped from the side of his mouth and rested at the corner of his smile.

"A crow. He's hurt. He needs help."

He nodded. "Where are the stars?" he asked eerily.

Standing close, I was staring at him. His skin seemed to be dripping from his face, like wax from a candle. The sickly white oozed away to reveal the black charcoal skull beneath. I watched as his nose came off and dropped to the ground. I was so out of it, it all seemed natural somehow.

"I knew your father," he said as his mouth came unhinged. "And I've been visiting your mother." He still spoke even as his mouth broke off and fell from his face.

"What do you want from me?" I asked.

"Give me the bird." I shook my head. "Give it to me. You can't heal it."

"No!" I yelled, and started to run. I stumbled down the side street. It seemed to go on forever. My legs were soft like jello, yet heavy like anchors. The sensation made me stagger along. Everything was bathed in vibrant colors, even in the dark—pink windows, purple cars, yellow sidewalks, red parking meters. I couldn't focus on moving too fast as the colors were so distracting. I was drawn to them and had to take them in.

I don't know how long I made myself stumble down the street before finally stopping beside two trash cans. Dropping between them and leaning my back against a concrete wall, I closed my eyes and passed out.

When I woke up, it was still dark. I shook my head to clear it and looked down at my bloody shirt, the vomit beside me, and the dead bird in my lap. I tried holding my hands over it, to see if I could bring it back, but I was so out of it, I couldn't do it. I set the bird down beside me, and I fell back asleep against the wall.

It was early in the morning when I woke up again. I still didn't feel right, but I managed to get up. The dead crow was right there at my feet. I felt like I had to try one more time to bring it back. Standing up, I set my hands over it. I felt shaky. I couldn't concentrate. I was useless to the bird. He wasn't coming back to life. That made me even shakier.

I left the dead crow and headed to Buddy's. I knocked on the door over and over. No one answered. I tried the handle. It was open. I went in.

Buddy was still in his bed. I stayed in the doorway of his bedroom when I said, "Hey, Buddy. Buddy. Wake up."

He turned toward me, his eyes squinty from sleep. "Carson." He rubbed at his eyes. "What's going on?" He stretched his arms up over his pillow and yawned.

"What did you give me last night in those brownies?" I asked.

He thought for a moment and then gave a laugh. "Good stuff?" he asked, lifting himself up and leaning back on his elbows.

I put my hands over my face and then closed them into fists over my mouth. "No," I admitted. "It was a really bad experience. And I still feel really weird."

He leaned over to look at the digital clock. "First time can be a bad trip," he said pushing his covers away and getting out of bed. Shirtless and wearing boxers, he grabbed jeans from the floor and put them on.

"What was it?" I asked. "Weed?"

He gave a mischievous smile as he shook his head. "Much better than weed."

"But I didn't like it at all. How come you guys didn't tell me it was in the brownies?"

"Carson," he narrowed his eyes at me as he buttoned and zipped his jeans. "Are you here to give me a hard time about this?" He threw his hands up. "You're the one who ran off. If you stayed with us, it would've probably been a good trip."

I wasn't about to argue with him. He was a lot bigger than me. And I was too out of it to make a good argument anyway.

"Listen," he said, putting his arm over my shoulder as he led me to the front door. "We just wanted to make your birthday special. Didn't turn out like we planned, but we tried."

I just nodded, realizing he wouldn't understand why I was upset.

"Next time you gotta stay with us, and I promise you'll like it."

I just nodded again and walked out the door.

I didn't want there to be a next time. I hated feeling out of control like that. The whole experience was disturbing, but one of the worst parts was not being able to use my healing power on the crow. I didn't ever want to take anything again that might inhibit my powers and risk the chance of losing them altogether. If I lost my gift, I'd have nothing. Just another screwed-up kid with no future. I didn't want to end up like that. I was a healer, and I was supposed to be a great one some day. I had that one thing that separated me from the other kids on the street. If I didn't have it, I'd probably want to numb my life like the rest of them. But I had it. And it kept me focused. It was my one shot in life and I didn't want to do anything to blow it.

Thirty-five

"You're even taller," was all Faris said as I approached the shop. He was nodding his head and giving me as much of a smile as his cigarette would allow.

"I'm fourteen now," I let him know, taking a seat on the crate beside him.

"Yeah, I know. I got your birthday present inside." He lifted his chin toward the shop. "Been sittin' in my station since your birthday," he said, getting up from his stool. He stretched his colorful arms as if he'd been sitting for quite some time and then walked to the door.

I stayed on the crate looking down at my hands, picking at my nails, wondering how he remembered it was my birthday when I wasn't even around to remind him.

"Nothin' much." He shrugged, coming back outside and tossing a small package to me. "Just something to say happy fourteen."

It was wrapped in blue paper with yellow writing that said "Happy Birthday." A yellow bow was tied on top. It struck me as funny—I tried to imagine Faris cutting the paper, wrapping and taping it, and then tying a bow. He must have noticed my smile.

"I had my lady friend help me out with the wrap job," he said.

"Yeah." I kind of laughed. "Wondered about that."

I tore the wrapping paper off and inside there was a black leather wallet with a twenty sticking out from the top. "Cool." I smiled. "Thanks, Faris."

"Yeah, happy birthday, kid." He sort of threw his hand toward me then let it fall into his lap. He leaned back against the wall and set his eyes on the traffic as the last of his cigarette hung from his lips. He didn't say any-thing—didn't ask how things were going with me. Maybe he was being cautious after our argument last time about my mom. I was glad he didn't ask. I didn't want to tell him what happened with Buddy and the guys. I knew I had to stay away from them for a while, but I wasn't sure I was ready to cut them off completely. They were my only friends. If Faris found out what they did, he would give me a hard time about them. I didn't want to tell him that my mom was in rehab, either. I'd tell him another time. There was something comforting that day about just being there and not having to deal with all the bad things that were going on in my life.

"Where's Beans today?" I asked.

"With his girlfriend."

"He's got a girlfriend?"

"Yeah. Her name's Kat. Cute girl. He's pretty into her."

There were some interesting people walking by on the sidewalk that day. There was a guy with a pretty impressive Mohawk and a street preacher calling out for all sinners to repent. Faris and I just watched the people, not having much to say, sharing yet another Hollywood afternoon together.

"I gotta go," I finally said after a while, getting up from the crate. "But I'll come back maybe next week or something." I was leaving for Washington DC in two days.

"Always good to see you, Carson," he said, putting his fingers to his forehead and giving me a mock salute.

"Tell Beans hey," I added.

"Will do."

"Oh, and thanks for the present," I said, holding up the wallet.

"Fourteen." He laughed a little—a smoker's laugh, sort of phlegmy. "These are the good years, Carson. These are the good ones."

They felt good sometimes, but I always thought getting older would be better. I wondered if Faris' teenage years were really that good for him, or if they were just a lot better than where he ended up.

Thirty-six

I was almost ready for my trip to Washington DC. There was just one thing I needed to do before I left. I found the business card in my drawer and made the call. Lolo's agent said she would get a hold of her for me. It was only a few hours later when Lolo called me back. She agreed to meet me at Nelson's bookstore.

Lolo wasn't wearing one of those tropical dresses this time. She wore jeans, boots, a silky blouse and designer sunglasses. She looked more Hollywood than Hawaiian.

We hadn't told Nelson we were coming. He wasn't there yet and the place was still closed. Standing together, leaning against the wall in front of the bookstore, we waited for him to show up. I told Lolo all about the people I had been healing at the head shop and all about the night with Veronica Sterling.

"I read in People Magazine about her going to an alternative healer." She took off her sunglasses, setting them on top of her head. Looking right into my eyes, in awe, she said, "That must be you, Carson."

I smiled. "I didn't know about the article. But, yeah, that was me."

"I am so proud of you." She leaned over and gave me a hug, really holding me tight. "Is that why you called to see me today?" she asked when she let me go. "To tell me about Veronica?"

"No. I wanted to see you today to let you know I'm leaving tomorrow," I said. "I'm flying to Washington DC, where my dad is buried. I'm going to try to bring him back."

"Carson." Lolo closed her eyes as her shoulders dropped. "You can't do that."

"But your grandmother did. With that boy. You said it could be done."

"No." She had a pained look on her face. "It can't be done."

"I just want to try it," I said. "If it doesn't work, then I'll know my limits. But I have to try."

"Does your mom know you're going?"

"No. She's in rehab. I can't talk to her for a month and a half. That's why I called you. I thought if I told you I'm really going, you might tell me more about how your grandma did it, so I'll know what I'm doing."

"Carson." Lolo squeezed up her face, and then took a deep breath. "I need to tell you the truth."

"About what?"

"Oh, Carson." She put her hands over her face like she wanted to hide. When she pulled her hands away she said, "Don't hate me, okay?"

"I won't," I said, wondering why she would ever think I'd hate her.

"I am just an actress. I'm not a healer." She looked at me waiting for a response. I didn't have one. I didn't understand what she was saying. "I was hired by your mom," she went on, "to play the part of a healer so that you would have a mentor. And I was auditioning for a part in a movie to play a healer." Now she was using her hands as she explained. "So your mom thought it would be a good idea for me to practice getting into character." She stopped her hands, lacing her fingers together and holding them under her chin. "I'm so sorry, Carson. I didn't think it would go so far."

My mind raced through the memories of my time with Lolo— the chanting, the intense spiritual connection we created, her knowledge of healing. There was no way it was all an act. "Okay, wait." I shook my head as if to clear away the crazy idea that she was a fake. "What do you mean?"

"The stuff I told you? It was just made up."

"What about the *mauiamu*? That's real. That's not made up."

She took a deep breath. "Your mom told me about the stars, and then together we created a name for it. The name was kind of random," she said, using her hands again, as if they helped keep the words coming. "The island of Maui came to my mind and then Juliette just threw a little extra sound at the end of it." I felt my face heating up.

"But what about the chant. How did you learn the chant?"

She cleared her throat. "Your mom found it on a CD here at Nelson's bookstore. She chose it because it fit my ethnicity."

"Everything you taught me was a lie?" I was so shocked, I felt like I had to reassess everything I thought I knew. "Does that mean my healing is all a lie?"

"No, no, no." She waved her hands. "*I* was a lie, Carson. But you being a healer is not a lie. I came into it thinking I was just practicing a part, but when I met you, I knew you were special. And I really believe you took everything I told you and molded it into something usable. I'm the one who was a fraud, but, Carson, you're as genuine as they get. You can really heal. It's just that I didn't have anything to do with it."

I pulled away from the wall and walked toward the street. I stood on the edge of the curb watching the traffic go by with only one thing in my mind—my mom was a liar.

"It doesn't change anything, Carson," Lolo said, approaching me by the curb. "You already had the gift before you met me. I only added details. Things that your mom thought might help you."

"Why are you telling me now?" I looked at her.

"I just felt like I had to tell you the truth so you don't go to this cemetery thinking you can bring your dad back. That was the only part that I made up on my own—about my grandmother. It wasn't true, Carson. My grandmother never brought back a dead boy. I just got carried away that first day with the story and your mom got mad at me for making it up. I was giving you the wrong direction. So after that day, I always kept to the script."

A script. An actress. A bunch of lies. "Why would my mom do that to me?"

"She didn't want you to quit," she tried to explain. "She said you threatened to quit healing and she didn't want to see you give it up. She thought that if she found you a mentor, you'd stick with it. Her intentions were good. She just didn't know a real healer—so she asked me to play one."

It was as if a brand-new corner of my brain opened up and there was sudden enlightenment. For the first time I could grasp what my mom had done to me—what Faris had meant when he said I lived in my mom's fantasy land.

"There's stuff that I believed about myself all my life." I was half thinking out loud and half talking to her. "What if it's all not even true? I mean, I trusted you a hundred percent. I trusted my mom a hundred percent. But you both lied. How do I know what's true anymore?"

She took hold of my hand. "You can still believe in yourself. What you do is true. The only thing that's not true is me."

That was when I pulled my hand away from her and started running. I could have too easily destroyed something with the way I was feeling inside. What I most wanted to get my hands on was my mom's room—I would have pulled her framed pictures from the walls and thrown them to the ground, taken her candles and broken them into pieces, ripped up her books, pounded in her walls. Instead, I ran and ran as far from the bookstore as I could get.

Thirty-seven

Too tired to want to destroy stuff in her room anymore, I went back to the bookstore. There was something I wanted to find. Nelson was there by the time I got back. I didn't say anything to him when I walked in. I just passed him at the counter and went straight to my mom's room. Exhausted from running, I threw myself on the lavender couch and just breathed. I looked around at the gods and goddesses on the walls and the unlit candles. I once thought everything in that room was magical. That day it all looked more like a sham.

"You know, she's the most unique woman I've ever known." Nelson was standing there in the doorway. His voice had the quality of a teacher or a preacher or someone with something important to say. "Your mother is more closely connected to the universe than anyone I've ever met." The fact that he came over to talk to me, and was saying things like that about my mom, I had the feeling he'd talked to Lolo. I let him go on anyway.

"The spirits love her just as much as people do," he said, "but sometimes the love gets too much for her and she feels overwhelmed in this life. That's why she drinks. She needs it to keep her grounded when the spirits get too strong." Now I was onto his motive. It wasn't about what had happened with Lolo. He was trying to make me feel better about my mom going to rehab.

"She's a drunk, Nelson." I could hear the rage coming back in my voice. "You make her sound like a saint. She fooled you, like she fooled me."

Nelson remained calm, taking a couple steps inside the room. He was wearing jeans, sandals, and an orange T-shirt that said BREATHE. "She didn't fool anyone," he said. "That was never her intention."

"You remember Lolo?" I asked.

"Of course." He nodded.

"You know she was just an actress, hired by my mom? To lie to me?"

"That's not true." Nelson came beside the couch but didn't sit down. He rubbed his hand over the bald spot on his head. "I know a little something about that. Your mom gave you Lolo because you asked her for a mentor, didn't you?"

I looked at him in shock. "How do you know about this?"

"She came to me for help with the research on what Lolo would teach you. I helped her find books so she could create direction for you. The information was authentic."

"So you were in on it too?"

"Your mother was trying to teach you how to use your gift," he said with his hands out. "She didn't want you to be overwhelmed in this life the way that she was."

"What else do you know?" I asked. "If my mom lied to me about Lolo, I want to know what else she made up."

"She didn't talk about her family life with me. Honestly. This was the only time she came to me for help."

I believed him. My mom wouldn't have told her secrets to this pathetic little man. I was done talking with Nelson. "Can I just have some time in here alone?" I asked.

"Okay." Nelson cleared his throat and stepped toward the door. "Okay. I'm, I'm sorry if—" but he couldn't seem come up with the rest of the sentence. I just nodded.

He closed the door and I lay back down on the lavender couch. I stared at the wall for a long time, trying to make sense of it all. Nothing had ever been conventional with my mom. Nelson might have been telling the truth about Lolo being a teacher instead of a complete fraud. It was possible my mom was genuinely trying to teach me something. I had told her I wanted some direction. But the part that bothered me most was that I now questioned the real truth about me. Did my mom really know I was a healer or was there a chance that she made it up to give me something to believe in? I started having doubts about my powers. Did I really heal her when I was little, or was that a setup for her great story—the one about me coming back to fulfill my ancient destiny? Could she have really orchestrated the whole thing?

I knew I healed people at Casper's place, so I didn't know how I could have built such power on top of a lie. It was a crazy idea that I could develop my gift just by my mom planting the idea in my head. She couldn't have just fabricated my destiny—could she? It was all so complicated. I couldn't be certain of anything anymore. If I stopped believing in myself, would I lose the gift? Was that all it took?

I got up from the couch. I didn't want all those thoughts going through my head, confusing me and making me doubt myself. I wanted to know the truth. I looked around the room, wondering where I might find what I'd come to get. I reached for the small dresser beside the couch. Shoved in a drawer with a few books and pens was exactly what I was looking for— a phone book. I turned to J. There it was, Jackson's name and a phone number. I ripped the page from the book, and put it in my pocket.

I knew what I had to do. There was only one person who might know the whole story from the beginning. When I finally made it back to the motel, I made the call. I got his recording, but I didn't leave a message. I would have to try him again tomorrow. From Washington DC.

Thirty-eight

I knew now that I couldn't bring back my dad. Lolo had made that clear when she told me she'd made up the whole story about her grandmother and the boy. But I went to Washington DC anyway. If I'd ever needed to be there, it was now. All I wanted was to stand before my father's grave and feel close to him. Touching the cold tombstone—the only thing left to tell the world he had been here—seemed almost as comforting as his unreachable hand.

Casper explained what I needed to do to get through an airport and how to catch a taxi. It was harder than it sounded, and the flight was longer than I'd imagined, but people were helpful when I asked questions. They were especially nice when I told them I was traveling to see my father for the first time. They all assumed it was my living father—except for the taxi driver.

"You're going to see your father at a cemetery?" he asked in a strange accent, though it wasn't so heavy that I couldn't understand what he was saying.

"Yes. Cemetery of Heroes. That's where he is," I said, buckling my seatbelt in the back of the taxi.

"Does he work there?" He sounded hopeful.

"No. He's buried there." I set my jacket on the seat beside me. "My dad is one of the heroes," I said, looking out the window at all the taxis and shuttles there in front of the airport and all the people going by with suitcases. It was probably the busiest place I'd ever seen.

"And you say it is called the Cemetery of Heroes?" the driver asked.

"Yes. My mom told me that's what it's called."

"Where is your mother?" He was looking at me through the rearview mirror, his eyes deep brown and kind.

"She's in rehab," I said. His eyes were still on me.

"You are here alone?"

"Yes."

"My friend," he turned around to face me, "you are too young to go at this alone."

"I'm not as young as I look," I said for what felt like the hundredth time. "I'm fourteen."

"I understand." He was gentle, turning back toward the steering wheel. "But fourteen is still too young to go alone to a cemetery for the first time to see your father."

"I saved up for a long time to get here." I tried to sound firm. "I'm here and I'm going." Looking directly into his eyes through the rearview mirror I said, "I can get another taxi if you don't want to take me."

His eyes stayed steady on me. "What is your name?"

"Carson. Why?"

"Carson, I will take you to see your father," he agreed. "But I will go with you into the cemetery. Okay?"

"You don't have to go with me."

"But I will," he said.

I didn't try to talk him out of it. It didn't sound so bad having someone there with me anyway.

"What's your name?" I asked, so I'd at least know something about him.

"Call me D," he said.

"Just D?"

"My full name could be too difficult for you to say. Dobroslav," he said with a roll of his tongue. I didn't think I could make that sound the way he did. I went ahead and called him D.

D asked me if I'd eaten dinner yet. I'd only had peanuts and soda on the plane, so I told him no. He said he was due for his break and he would like to take me to an early dinner. I felt pretty lucky that of all the taxis I could have gotten in, this one probably had the nicest driver.

We went to a restaurant and sat together in a red vinyl booth, eating hamburgers and fries. We talked the whole time. He told me about his wife that he had just married and the baby on the way. He was both nervous and excited about becoming a father. I told him all about my life and the whole story about my dad. His eyes went sad when I told him every-thing. D was a good listener. For being practically a stranger, he acted like he really cared. That didn't happen a lot in life. Strangers didn't usu-ally waste their time on kids like me. I told him I could tell he would be a good dad when his own kid was born.

I waited inside the restaurant, finishing my dessert, while D went out and called his dispatcher to get directions to the cemetery. Once he got them, he came back inside, paid for the check, and said we were ready to go.

It was about a half-hour drive to the cemetery. When we drove up, I pressed my face against the window to check it out. It was small and old-looking. It had huge gray tombstones—cement crosses, angels, big blocks, and a whole variety of shapes there on the grass. It kind of looked like a life-size chess game, but with way more pieces.

"Is this where all military heroes are buried?" I asked D as we pulled into the parking lot.

"There is the Arlington National Cemetery. It is much bigger. This one, though, also has elite heroes. It sounds like your father was one of those."

"Where's the sign that says Cemetery of Heroes?" I asked. "That one," I pointed to the front, "says Sacred Heart Cemetery. I think we're at the wrong one."

"Sacred Heart is the official name," D said, "but it is the Cemetery of Heroes to those here in Washington DC who know about it." It was a good thing D was there to help me. I realized I would have been lost on my own.

The sun hadn't completely set, but even with a little light still out, the place was eerie. I stayed close to D as we walked to the main building. No one was there to help us, but D found a book with grave listings. "What was your father's name?" he asked.

"Donovan Calley," I said.

He paged through the book while I looked around the small building we were in. It was pretty rundown and bare. A few old, religious pictures hung on the walls and there were some folding chairs facing a big brown desk. D was leaning over that desk reading through the grave listings. The place was a disappointment to me. I thought a hero, who did great things for his country, deserved a much nicer cemetery. I told D what I thought. He didn't seem to have a good answer to that, but just tried to smile and said, "Come with me."

We walked along a dirt path, the great tombstones all around us. I read the names of dead people as we passed them and wondered if all of their spirits were still there, watching us. I could almost feel them as an electrified sensation ran through me. It was probably the most scared I'd ever felt in my life. I was grateful to have D there with me.

We were deep along the path when I heard rustling noises over by the trees. I slowed down and D turned back. "You okay, Carson?"

"Do you hear that?" I asked, stopping. "Over by the tree?" I pointed.

D walked toward the noise. He was a big man, but I didn't think that mattered when it came to ghosts. My heart was pounding as he walked further away from me and closer to the noise. I stayed on the path, surrounded by the gray tombstones, while he was somewhere behind the trees. Standing motionless and holding my breath, I heard a loud bang followed by a screeching cry. I screamed and started running back toward the main building.

"Carson," I heard D calling after me. "It's okay, it's okay." When he'd caught up to me on the path, I was crying. I felt completely spooked, completely out of control. I didn't want to be there anymore. I wanted to go home.

D put his arm around my shoulder. "It's okay, it was just some crows by a trash can. I kicked the can and they flew away. That's all it was. Just crows." I wiped at my eyes. "Do you want to leave?" he asked. "Is this too much for you?"

The crows were here; maybe to comfort me. I put my hand on my crow tattoo and held onto it. "No," I said in the strongest voice I could muster. "Let's keep going. I want to see where my dad is."

Still scared but trying to be courageous, I stayed close behind D as we continued along the path. We finally came to a tombstone that stood alone. It was just the traditional rounded shape, but it was one of the biggest. It was set in front of a huge tree. D stood before it and said, "Your father is here."

This was it. The moment I'd been waiting for. I took a few steps and stood beside D. I read the engraving: "A coward dies a thousand deaths, a soldier dies but once." But there was no name, no dates.

"How do you know this is my father's? His name's not on it." I was shivering, but not because it was cold.

"It was in the book," D explained. "It said Donovan Calley in the book and this is exactly where it said he was. Maybe the tombstone was made before they identified him."

D stepped back so that I could have a moment there at my dad's grave. I knelt down and put my hand on the cold gravestone. "Dad?" I said looking down at the ground. "Is this really you?" I hoped that some great sign would come, or even just a rush of comfort would fill me up inside. But instead all I felt was the fear of being in a cemetery surrounded by dead people.

Had I still believed I had the power to bring my father back, I don't think I would have even tried it. I was way too scared. I couldn't find any peace, inspiration, or comfort being there at my father's grave. I couldn't even think about my dad. All I could do was stay as motionless as possible, listening to the silence, waiting for a noise to tell me one of the ghosts had showed up.

When the noise finally came—a wild rustling in the tree above us—I jumped up, screamed and ran. My whole body was electrified with fear as I sprinted all the way back to the parking lot. It felt like forever as I made my way passed all the tombstones, certain I was being watched by the spirits who lived there. I only hoped they were just watching me and wouldn't grab me and hurt me.

When I got to the taxi, I pulled at the door handle over and over trying to get in. D showed up quickly. He unlocked the door saying, "Carson, it was just a squirrel. There was a squirrel in the tree."

I didn't care what it was. I just wanted to leave that place and never go back.

D drove me to my hotel by the airport. He tried talking to me on our drive. I said nothing back. I didn't want him to hear my voice and know that I'd been crying. "I am sorry," he said when we pulled up to the hotel. He was turned around, looking at me in the backseat. "I am sorry it wasn't what you had hoped for."

"It's okay," I said. "At least I finally made it here." I shrugged, keeping my head low.

"You are the bravest boy I ever met. I hope my son grows to be like you." I tried to smile. It probably looked fake but it was all I had. "One day," he said, and then pointed his finger at me, "you will be the hero."

"Thanks, D," I said, even though I didn't believe him. I dropped my head, and got out of the cab. He had told me I didn't have to pay anything.

I didn't look back at him. I went into the hotel to check in. It was only when they hassled me at the front desk and wouldn't let a kid my age check in alone that I realized D hadn't driven away. He came to check in for me.

I just wanted to leave and get back home to Hollywood. I wasn't even courageous enough to try and go back to see my father the next day when it was light out. I never wanted to walk through another cemetery again. I may have come from great blood, but lately, it wasn't looking like my dad's greatness got passed down me. After Lolo's exposé, my healing had been thrown into question, and now even my honor was questionable. I knew I should have gone back to pay my respect to my father and spend more time with him. I owed him at least one more visit while I was there, but I was just too scared to do it. Unlike my dad, I was probably going to die a thousand deaths. My courage was all gone.

Thirty-nine

Jackson was standing by baggage claim when I came down the escalator after the plane landed. It was the first time I'd actually seen him face to face. He was old, almost as old as Faris. He still wore his long gray hair in a ponytail. Tall and thin, he was casual in his T-shirt, jeans, and Birkenstocks.

"Carson," he said. When I approached, he was hesitant at first, but then put his arms out awkwardly, as if to hug me. I carefully kept my distance.

"Hi." My voice was cool.

I had called Jackson from a payphone when I first arrived in Washington DC. I was still hoping to get answers at that point. I still wanted to know what else my mom had lied to me about, so I asked Jackson if he would pick me up when I got back. After my experience at the cemetery, I didn't even care anymore about what Jackson might be able to tell me. I felt so defeated, nothing mattered too much anymore.

"I'm glad you called," he said. He looked at me with the beginnings of a smile, but then dropped his eyes. I stared at him, waiting for him to say something. His eyes stayed lowered, keeping that smile.

"I can't believe what a handsome young man you've grown into," he finally said looking back up at me. "You got your mother's looks."

"How can you be sure?" I muttered. "You never knew my dad."

He took a deep breath and his face grew solemn. "You called me. You asked me to come, but it's obvious you're not happy to see me," he said. He kind of squinted as he looked at me. Was it painful for him to look at me? Did I remind him too much of my mother, the woman who must have complicated his life?

"Why would I be happy to see you?" I just felt like speaking the truth. "You're the guy who made my mom miserable for years. It's probably because of you that she drinks too much and now she's stuck in rehab." People nearby, waiting for their luggage, were drawn into our conversation. Jackson looked embarrassed. "I don't like you very much, but I didn't know who else to call."

He nodded. "There's more to the story than you know." Jackson's voice was almost at a whisper. "When we leave here, I will tell you what you want to know."

"I do know the part where you were married while you were dating my mom."

He looked around. Plenty of people had to have heard.

"It was complicated." He spoke softly. "Come here," he said, walking off to a side area, away from the crowd. I followed him. "We have three children." He tried to explain. "My wife is a good woman. I couldn't leave her. Your mom knew that from the beginning."

"Then why didn't you just let my mom go?"

"I couldn't. I loved her."

"You're so selfish. Do you even know how selfish you sound?"

"Yes, I know how it sounds, but it wasn't like that. I helped support you two," he said as if that might make everything okay.

"Yeah, you gave her money so she wouldn't tell your wife about you guys," I said.

"That's not why I gave her money."

"Oh, so there's some honorable reason you paid her?"

"Yes," he said. "I had to support my son."

"Your son." I glared at him.

"My son." He put his hands out toward me.

"Me? No way. My dad was—"

"Me," he said.

I stared at Jackson and tried to muster as much calm and composure as I could as Jackson told me the truth about my birth. He let me know that the military guy in the Special Forces who could kill a crow with his bare hands never existed. Jackson had been in Vietnam, but that was about it. It was all a lie. My mom knew I'd eat it up, every last crumb, as the lonely fatherless boy I was. She made sure that my father was a hero, better than most dads. Mine was almost a superhero. He could do no wrong. My mom spoke of his greatness. If I came from great blood, it only made sense that I would grow to be a great man. But it was now looking like my greatness was as much of a lie as my great father.

"She even lied about my dad?" I said, lifting my chin up high so that the water gathering in my eyes wouldn't run down my cheeks.

"She just wanted to protect you. Your mother loves you so much."

"She loves me so much, she just kept lying to me?"

"Look at you, Carson. Look what you've become. I know what you've already done at such a young age. Your mother told me when you were born that you'd do something big with your life. She would make sure of that."

"You give her the credit for what I've become?" My voice grew loud again.

"Most kids are raised with limits." He spoke quietly. "They're given small, realistic dreams. You had the kind of mom that didn't give you limits. She gave you the sky."

I could feel the rage coming. "But she didn't give me a father. I would have given up the fucking sky for a father." Even with our distance from the crowd, people were staring.

"I'm sorry, Carson." His forehead grew deep lines.

I had to look away from him. I didn't want to know the truth anymore. I wanted to erase it from my mind. I suddenly wished my mom were there to give me one of her stories.

"Carson?" he said. "Are you okay?"

I was standing there with my hands over my face when I felt his hand on my shoulder. I didn't want him to touch me. I pushed his hand away, and I started throwing my fists at him with everything I had. I didn't care about keeping it under control. My rage fit the moment—it felt right. I couldn't stop. I hated him. I hated what he told me. I tried to hit him harder and harder. He didn't even hit back. Instead, he pulled me toward him in an embrace that restrained me.

"Carson. Carson." His voice remained calm and he was strong enough to eventually get a hold of me. I tried to wriggle out from his restraint—I twisted and squirmed and struggled with all I had, but he had more. He was bigger than me. He wasn't letting me go.

"You have your mother's fire." His voice was still oddly calm as he forcefully took hold of me. He squeezed harder and then I just stopped fighting it. And I let my father hold me tightly in his arms. My body grew limp. I couldn't move. I stayed there paralyzed by this unlikely embrace.

Security came to check on us. Jackson told them he was having a dispute with his son. I yelled that I didn't want to be his son, and yet I let Jackson lead me to his car, just to get out of there. I cried the entire ride back to the motel. Jackson didn't even try talking to me anymore. He let me stay in my sadness alone. When we pulled up, I jumped out of the car without another word for Jackson.

I ended up walking down Hollywood Boulevard instead of going to my room. My walk was brisk, my vision blurred by tears. I felt smothered by a terrible loneliness. I had that same feeling I'd had as a kid, by myself in a motel room, scared and alone in the dark. But as a kid, I knew my mom would always come back, crawl into bed and put her arms around me. This time she was locked up in some rehab facility. She couldn't come back to me.

I walked the streets with the fresh knowledge that my father was actually alive, but he was not at all a hero. It came with the realization that even D, my taxi-driver friend, had lied to me. There was no Cemetery of Heroes, but after hearing my story, D probably didn't want to let me down. He did what he could to be sure the poor fatherless boy would believe he'd found his dad.

Did I appear so naïve and so pathetic that adults felt like they had to protect me with make-believe stories? Was it because I was small for my age that they thought I was too young for the truth? Or did they all think that my life was so bad, they were compelled to sugarcoat it with comforting lies? The problem was, now that I was seeing through the lies, it wasn't all that comforting anymore.

The Hollywood Healer. The son of a warrior. None of it was true. I wandered the streets, lost like some homeless kid stumbling along, mumbling, crying, cut off from the world around me. I made my way to the lot behind the Fonda Theater, hoping my friends would be there. I didn't even care about what they'd done on my birthday. I just wanted to be with them.

It was still light out. Buddy and the guys weren't there yet. Alone, I collapsed to the ground leaning against the dumpster, letting this profound loneliness get the best of me. I took a sharp rock from the ground and scratched it over my black crow tattoo, trying to erase it. I scratched and scratched until the blood hid the tattoo, covering up the lie of my father.

Forty

I didn't want to go anywhere. For three days I stayed alone in my motel room eating nothing but some saltine crackers and peanuts. During the day I lay in bed watching TV or losing myself in my old books. Anything just to be alone. But at night, after falling asleep, the ghosts came. Every night in my motel room, the dead black crow that I couldn't heal the night of my birthday came back to me. It would scream at me in my sleep until my dad would show up—the dad I used to believe in. He wore a military uniform, but it was all ripped up. Everything else about him was vague. While the crow screamed, my dad would sneak up behind it and kill it. Once the crow was dead, my dad would disappear. And a light would come on. And my mom would be there.

"Look at you," she said in a pained whisper the first time she came to me. "You're growing into a man. A gorgeous, healthy, perfect young man." She brought her hands to my face, her fingertips traveling down my cheeks. Her attention was intent and sober. Her eyes were sponges, taking in every detail of me.

"Mom," I cried, and the urgency of my own voice pulled me from my sleep. I woke alone in the motel room. Shivering and disoriented, I kept my eyes on the door, wondering what time she would finally come home.

The next night, after the black crow had been killed, she came to me again. We were at the Starlight. I couldn't see her face this time. I only saw her cinnamon hair and her turquoise dress that looked like it was made of scarves. She stood outside the door leaning against the balcony railing, while I stood in the doorway of our second-story motel room. "Mom," I pleaded.

The wind blew at her hair and teased the scarves of her dress. "I love you more than you know."

"Then why all the lies?"

"They weren't all lies, Carson."

"You told me I came from a great dad. And it was only Jackson. And what about the healing? I believed you. And now I don't know if I can do it anymore."

The wind grew more aggressive and her hands gripped the wrought-iron railing behind her. "Of all things, the healing—that's the one that has proven true."

"Did you really know?" I asked. "Or did you make stuff up to get me to believe it?"

"A magician never tells her secrets," she muttered, turning her back to me. She leaned out over the railing as the wind went wild. She seemed to revel in the power of the wind until it picked her up and took her away. I watched her go, screaming myself to wakefulness.

The next night, my mom came back again. She wore a white robe, like an angel.

"Please," I said, picking up our conversation from the night before. "Just for once, tell me the truth. Were you really a psychic? Did you really know about my power? Or did you manipulate me into believing stuff, like you did with your clients?"

"If I answer you," she said, her voice like warm vanilla, "will you let it go?"

I nodded.

"So you've narrowed my choices to a psychic or a manipulator? That's it?" She threw in a tired little laugh.

I nodded again.

She wrapped her arms tightly around herself. "I was both, Carson." I could see her face now. Her eyes were sad, her smile sorry. "I was both," she said again.

As I stared at her, I could see something black peeking out from her sides. Two great black wings, the wings of a crow, unfolded from behind her. She flapped them and suddenly began shrinking. She shrunk to the size of a bird. I watched as she flew up and perched herself on the wrought-iron railing. She looked peaceful and content. Until he came, in his ripped uniform, and swiftly killed her with a single swipe of his hand.

I jumped up from the bed, horrified by the death I'd just witnessed. I felt out of touch, out of control, and I needed to find some sanity. I couldn't take the dreams anymore. I had to break the spell of isolation and leave the motel room. I needed more food than saltines and peanuts.

I came back to real life by walking the streets of Hollywood, taking in the sights and sounds and smells of the city. I immersed myself back into the world so the loneliness wouldn't drive me crazy. I didn't interact with anyone. I just quietly blended in with them there on the sidewalks, finding my place within the great pedestrian wave.

Forty-one

I went back to the head shop to let Casper know I was done healing. I told him what had happened and how my gift was just a lie. He listened to what I said, but didn't respond right away. His response came after he took out the appointment book and opened it for me to see the list.

"Healing them will help heal you. You committed to these people, Carson," he spoke with firmness yet patience. "I understand that you've found out some rough truths about your life. I'm sorry about that, but you still need to follow through on these commitments. I won't add anyone else to the schedule for now, but I don't want to see you quit on people who are counting on you."

"But you don't get it. I can't do it anymore. I can't heal them."

"Carson, I believe you can," he said with a pained smile. "You need to get back to work so you can find yourself again. Will you just try? Will you let them come in and just try to help them?"

"I'll keep these appointments," I gave in with a shake of my head. "Just to show you that I can't do it anymore."

The following day they came in. One by one I took the clients into my room, but I couldn't get myself to use the phony chant anymore, and there was no way I was going to call forth the bogus *mauiamu*. Instead, I tried just holding out my hands and closing my eyes as I prayed to the gods that they'd continue granting me miracles—even though I didn't believe in myself anymore.

I was a failure. I couldn't heal any of them. After four unsuccessful tries, I told Casper I was done. He had to send the fifth person home. I stayed there in the turquoise room as Casper got on the phone to cancel the rest of my appointments. I turned off the lights and locked the door. I put in the CD that Harper Dee, the indie rock singer, had given me months ago. I sat against a wall and listened to her voice that had once taken me so high. This time I let it comfort me in my low. I couldn't dance like I'd danced the last time. I only swayed my head from side to side against the wall, remembering that exhilarating beginning of my healing career as it now came to an end.

Without a job anymore, I couldn't afford staying alone at the motel. Casper let me move into his place that was just above the shop. He wanted me to stay with him because he was convinced he could help me through what he called my blockage. I'd blown most of the money I'd made healing, so he supported us with his regular business from the head shop. I stayed inside the apartment upstairs watching TV most of the day. I still didn't want to go anywhere. I was too depressed to see anyone. But at least Casper was there with me and he brought me food, so I didn't have those nightmares anymore.

I was at my lowest point and yet Casper's belief in me was stronger than ever. Every night before going to sleep, Casper would give me a sort of pep talk, assuring me that my inability to heal was temporary—a mental block.

"Greatness isn't easy to maintain," he told me one night sitting on the edge of the couch that I slept on. His dreads were pulled back into a ponytail. In the dim light, his soft, pale skin made him look like an angel. "All great men must stumble on their way to success."

"I can't believe you still think I'm on my way to success." I tried to laugh. "I'm fake. You know the whole story. I thought I had something special that I don't actually have."

He shook his head. "You couldn't have accomplished all that you did without having something special."

"They just thought they were being healed. If you tell someone something with one hundred percent confidence," I said remembering my mom's words, "you can get them to believe anything. Like the emperor's new clothes—they saw what they wanted to see."

"So I just *wanted* my hearing to come back and so that's how I can hear again? Veronica Sterling just *wanted* her cancer to go away? It's no illusion. We were all healed because of you. I know that you know this deep inside. Yes, your mother lied to you. Yes, you believed a lot of things that you now know are not true. But don't let go of this one thing that is true.

Don't give in to this crazy belief that just because your mother lied, your healing was also a lie."

I let Casper talk and talk, but I wasn't buying into his logic, and I couldn't get inspired by his pep talks. I was too down to let him pull me up. I was mourning the death of the person I thought my father was, and the person I thought I was. I just wanted to stay in a place of darkness and sorrow. It felt like that was where I needed to be for a while. I shut myself off from that spiritual source that had made me heal. I wouldn't connect to that higher place even though I still felt drawn to it. Sometimes I'd have an overwhelming desire to take myself into a prayer-like state and experience again the power that made me feel whole, but I resisted. Even without my belief in myself, the light inside of me didn't go away. I just learned to ignore it.

Forty-two

After a week, Casper made me go back to school. He wouldn't let me stay locked up in his apartment anymore, doing nothing but watching TV. He said either I'd go back to school, or he would take me to see a psychiatrist.

The first day back, Rose approached me right when she saw me in the halls. I dreaded what she was going to say or do to me, but she ended up being surprisingly nice. "Where have you been?" she asked. "I've been looking for you."

"I've been sick," I said, wondering why she was looking for me.

"If you're sick, why didn't you just heal yourself?"

"I don't do that anymore," I said, walking away to my class.

"Yes, you do," she said, walking with me. "Who would be so stupid just to give up power like that?"

"I never really had the power," I said.

She laughed, hitting me with her elbow. "Shut up," she said. "Anyway, I was wondering what you're doing tonight. I have to babysit just for like a couple hours." She smiled, her voice growing a little softer, like the way it did that day on West Cherry. "Wondered if you'd come over and hang out with me."

Her words and that soft voice brought a tiny spark to my darkened state. I was still attracted to her in a tortured kind of way. I knew she wasn't the right girl for me, but she was perfect for the moment. A miserable girl for my miserable life.

I felt like the old Carson that night, heading to the West Cherry house again, hoping to get another kiss from Rose. It was the happiest I'd been in a long time. When I got there, the baby was already asleep in his crib and his sister was asleep in her room. Rose was sitting on the couch watching TV. I went and sat close beside her. "I'm glad you invited me over," I told her, putting my arm up on the couch just behind her.

"Don't get the wrong idea," she said, moving away from my arm. "I asked you over because I need a favor."

"There's no way Faris will do it," I said. "I already tried everything." I should have known she just wanted something from me.

"No, not a tattoo. I want you to heal me. You know, that voodoo thing you do." She wiggled her fingers around mockingly.

"I'm done with that," I said, folding my arms.

"You did it for all those other people at that head shop. I know all about what you did there. I even know people who went to you." It seemed that most people in town knew someone who had come to me. Casper told me that even though I quit, people still talked about me. "So you'll see strangers, but not me." She gave me a sour look. "What, do you want me to *pay* you?"

"It's not about the money." I looked down at my hands. "I just don't do that anymore. I actually don't even have the power I thought I had."

She looked upward and pursed her lips, blowing out air. "Okay, forget it. Maybe you should just go then." She got up from the couch and opened the front door for me.

"Wait," I said. "Are you sick or something?"

"No." She sounded frustrated.

"Then what do you want me to heal?"

"That thing I do when I blink and I can't—" She stopped. Giving a snotty look, she said, "Why am I even telling you? You're not gonna help me. Why don't you just go." She was still holding the open door.

Of all people, Rose was the last person I would have expected to believe in me.

"Before I go, can you just tell me why you think I can heal you?"

"The baby." Her stiffened hands bounced with her words. "After you did your voodoo thing on him, he got better."

Her belief in me was unexpectedly inspiring. "This is totally weird. I would have never guessed that you would ask me to—"

"Forget it. Seriously, Carson." She was shaking her head. "Just get out. You're still a loser, just like you were before. You couldn't get me the tattoo. Now you won't heal me."

"Why do you treat me like this?" I raised my voice.

"Because you're a loser," she said again.

"You have no idea what I've been through," I said, almost shouting.

"And you have no idea what I've been going through for years," she shouted back and then her eyes started blinking uncontrollably. She threw her hands over her eyes. "Fuck you for not even trying!" she cried from behind her hands.

Rose walked away from the door and switched on the bright lights in the kitchen. I was stunned for a moment. I stared at the light and could feel it seeping into me, as if feeding something inside of me. I went to the kitchen and took it in as I watched Rose walk over to the sink and lean on it. Her back was to me, but I could see by the way her shoulders shook that she was crying.

At that moment, standing behind her and watching her cry, I knew I had the power to make it go away. I absolutely knew. Anger was replaced with compassion and confidence. I suddenly felt that old certainty that used to fuel my gift. It was like waking up from one of those dreams where you're stuck in one spot and even if you try to run you can't seem to go anywhere. I'd woken up. I was free. I could move again. My mom may have been a liar, Lolo may have been a fraud, my dad may not have been my blood link to greatness, the *mauiamu* and the chant may have been gimmicks, but despite all that, I knew without a doubt that I could still heal Rose.

"*E ho mai.*" My voice cracked as I began chanting the words I thought I'd never say again.

"What are you saying?" she said, sniffling.

I moved closer to her and placed my hands over Rose's head as I went on. "*Ka ike mai luna mai e.*" A swarm of light rushed through me and I could feel the tiny stars gather in my hands. I had to catch my breath as I fell back into the old spiritual sensation that took me high. I was alive again, in the way that felt most natural to me.

As the thousands of stars left my hands and took to Rose, I didn't care whether or not they had a name. *Mauiamu* was a fabricated term, but the stars themselves were as real as the hands they came from. The facts couldn't deny the feeling. And I would no longer deny who I was. By the time the healing was done, Rose was in tears. She tried to wipe them away and act like her usual callous self, but the act didn't work.

"You sounded like a freak." She tried to laugh. "With that 'ikky-my-aye' song." She sniffled, wiping her eyes on her sleeve. I just watched her, the hardened girl slightly softened. "But it's cool." She gently hit my shoulder with the back of her hand and smiled. "That you did your voodoo thing for me. I—" she shrugged "—appreciate it."

I just nodded. We looked at each other for a few moments. I thought maybe a hug would be appropriate, but I didn't feel it in me and apparently neither did she. A smile and a goodbye was enough.

I left Rose that night unexpectedly inspired. Apparently she'd been placed in my life for a reason. She was the one person who could rouse the kind of emotion in me that would make me stumble back into my real self. My mind would have never let me willingly go back. It took an emotional disaster to get me back on track. And that's about all Rose was for me.

When I got back to the apartment I went into Casper's room to tell him that I could heal again. I told him exactly what had happened with Rose. When I was through, he hugged me. Unlike Rose, a hug really meant something from Casper. "We're back in business," he said. "When do you want to start?"

"Whenever," I shrugged. "I'm ready."

"They've been waiting for you, Carson," he said. "You stopped believing in yourself, but the people of Hollywood never stopped believing in you."

The next day, Casper had four people to see me. And more the day after that, and even more the day after that.

Forty-three

I was alone in the turquoise room, lighting the candles along the walls. I took my time lighting them since I had over twenty minutes before my first appointment. I'd been back for two weeks now and it was clear that my hands had recaptured their magic.

My room there in the head shop was like a church to me. It was the place where I felt spiritually connected to that great presence outside as well as inside of me. I couldn't explain the presence, and I couldn't figure out how I'd managed to get in touch with it. I only knew that I didn't feel complete unless I acknowledged it. The time I had spent denying my gift had been a really dark time for me. I never wanted to go there again. Even if it meant I needed to accept that my mom's lies helped guide me to where I ended up, I had no choice. My gift called me and I had to listen.

Once all the candles were lit, I took one of the Mexican blankets to the center of the room. All alone, I sat and closed my eyes. I took deep breaths as I tried to clear my mind of all thoughts. I just wanted to feel the comfort of being in this space. As I breathed, my mind emptied, and I felt overwhelmed by a great feeling, familiar but in some way new. It seemed to travel from my heart and radiate outward, spilling itself throughout my entire body. Every inch of me was overwhelmed by a great wave of emotion that I recognized as gratitude.

"Carson," I heard from behind me and turned toward the sound. I opened my eyes and I saw Casper's head peeking through the partially open door. Two of his dreads hung there in the opening. As he leaned in further, all the pale bundles of matted hair came forward. "Your first appointment is here early. Did you want her to come in now, or should I tell her to wait?"

Still feeling the wave of emotion inside, I asked for a few more minutes. With a nod, Casper closed the door and left me alone a little longer.

I had healed so many strangers. I'd called forth the thousands of tiny stars to heal everything from a simple rash to cancer. I'd given people hope. I'd given them relief. My destiny called for a lot of giving. At times it was draining and chaotic, and even confusing, yet I was grateful for this path I'd agreed to take. Somehow all that giving had a way of giving back to me.

I got up from the floor and looked around the room once more. It appeared ready for the day. But just before leaving the room, I stopped there at the door, setting my eyes on one of the candle flames. I was fourteen years old, and I was already one hundred percent certain what I was meant to do with my life. It wasn't always going to be easy, but I knew it would satisfy me more than anything else.

For some reason I was chosen, though I probably wasn't even the best man for the job. I didn't come from great blood like I'd once thought—my mom was a drunk and a liar, my dad was a cheater and a liar. I didn't have their same flaws, but I did have my own. These same hands that healed were sometimes compelled to be destructive. I'd managed to get some control over the urges when I ran myself to exhaustion, but I didn't know if those episodes of rage would ever completely go away. Maybe the gods gave them to me to keep me humble, to realize that I was flawed even as I had great power.

Whatever the reason may have been, I'd done some pretty bad things. I couldn't go back and redo them, but I finally opened up to Casper about it all, and asked for his advice. He suggested how I might make up for my crimes. I made enough money to pay for what I'd destroyed—the motel's storage closet, the Italian restaurant's chef statue, the windows on La Cienega. With Casper's help, I left anonymous notes along with cash at these places to pay for damages. It didn't make my crimes go away, but it felt like a step in the right direction.

Taking one last deep breath in the turquoise room, as the gratitude continued to swell, I turned away from the candle and opened the door.

"Hello, Carson," she said, standing there, squinting her eyes, as if she were protecting them from the sun—from her son.

"Mom!" It came out with such unexpected happiness. I planned to be mad at her when she came back, but without a chance to plan, I only felt the joy of finally seeing her again.

She came into the room and hugged me. Her hair smelled fruity, like mangoes or peaches—like it did when I was a kid.

"When did you get out?" I asked as I pulled away to look at her. Her cinnamon hair was tamed by a long braid. No makeup, no jewelry, she just wore a loose white dress. She looked clean, like she belonged on a soap commercial.

"I got out today," she said, her eyes sober. "Jackson picked me up and brought me right to you."

"Jackson?" I asked. Now the mad feeling came on.

"I know." She dropped her eyes and gave a rapid nod. "He told me that you know the truth about him."

"And I talked to Lolo," I said. "She told me the truth about her, too."

She looked back up at me. Her mouth opened, but she didn't say anything.

She dropped her head in her hands and slouched her shoulders. "They don't give you a manual at the hospital when you have a baby," she said into her hands. "No one tells you what you're supposed to do."

She eased down to sit on the floor, folding her legs under her white dress, still hiding her face. "I had to make it up as I went. And I know I screwed up." She tried to look up at me when she said this but then put her face right back into her hands. "I screwed up so much, but I still got this amazing kid." I could tell by her voice that she was crying now. "I don't deserve you, Carson."

"Mom," I said, going to her and sitting on the floor, facing her.

"I should've ended up with a screwup like me," she went on. "That would have been just. But the gods didn't see it that way." Now she looked at me, her eyes all wet. "Instead of a screwup, they gave me you." She put her hands out toward me. "Don't you understand?" Leaning forward, she reached for my hands and squeezed them with her cold hands. Her voice went soft as she said, "I had to give you back something better than what I really was."

She let go of my hands and started crying so much, she couldn't talk. I was afraid her first day out of rehab like this would drive her to drink again. I didn't care so much about making her explain all the lies right then. I just wanted to see her calm down and get through her first day back in real life.

I held my hands out to her, closed my eyes, and brought out the stars. It was the most natural healing experience of all for me—taking care of my mom. That was how my gift started, and it was something I would keep doing as long as she needed me. I could be mad at her, and disappointed in her, but she was still my mom. I had some tough questions for her, and I would ask them when the time was right. But for the moment, I just wanted to reach out my hands to her and help her get healthy. Even if she was kind of a messed-up mom, she was all I had.

When her crying stopped and she calmed down, she stayed there on the floor, facing me. She put her hands up over her mouth, as if in prayer, and just looked at me. She was proud of me, her eyes said. I could tell that was what they were saying. And in a way, looking into her completely sober eyes, I was proud of her, too.

Forty-four

I got on my skateboard one day and headed over to House of Freaks. It had been way too long since I'd gone back to see Faris.

I sat on the old crate and Faris was on his stool beside me. He listened to me talk, like he always had over the years, while watching the traffic on the street and the people on the sidewalk. He never looked at me, but I still knew he was taking everything in. That's how Faris was. We sat for a long time. I opened up to him and told him everything. Sometimes I noticed him nodding his head, and then other times he'd give it a slow shake. He went through several cigarettes and a Diet Coke.

"Holy shit!" I heard the familiar voice from down the street. He was walking toward me with a bit of a slouch to his swagger. He was holding hands with a petite redhead. "The boy came back. Thought we lost him to another tattoo shop. Thought maybe he finally found someone to ink his thirteen-year-old girlfriend."

My lips pulled to one side as they held back a smile. "Hey, Beans."

"Car-son," Beans sang. "Where you been, man?"

We shook hands. "Around," I said.

"This is Kat." He introduced me to his girlfriend.

"Hey, Carson." She reached her hand out to me. "Glad to finally meet you."

She was really cute, dressed all girly in a lacey pink dress with pastel-colored tattoos up her arms. She wore thick fake lashes, red lipstick, a diamond nose ring, and rubies in her eyebrows. She was a perfect match for Beans.

The two of them stood beside the crate and talked with Faris and me for a bit and then went inside. That was when Faris finally had something to say about all that I'd told him. "You know, people come into the shop here and talk about the things you can do. Everyone in town knows about the Hollywood Healer."

"Do you believe in me yet?" I asked.

"I've always believed in you. I always thought you'd do great things."

"No, I'm talking about my power," I said, looking straight ahead. "Do you believe I can really heal?"

He paused to light another cigarette. "What can I say? You got people claiming they've been healed by you of real serious diseases," he said with a shake of his head. "You say you really got this gift. And I know you. You're no liar."

That was as good as a yes to me. I didn't know what to say so I just sat there, looking across the street at the radio station. No protestors were there that day. The sun was bright, the air was warm. It didn't feel like the kind of day for conflict. There was a sense of peace in the air.

"Your mom did okay by you," Faris said. His words made me look back at him. "Yeah, I know it was hard for you, her being on the bottle and all, and hooking you up with that bogus actress. But you turned out fine under the circumstances."

"What did you think when I came here with that stupid story about that superhero kind of dad, flying a one-man plane, and killing a crow with his bare hands?" I tried to laugh like someone old enough to know better.

"I knew the story was a bunch of shit, but since she felt like she had to come up with it, I figured the truth must be pretty bad."

"You knew it was a bunch of shit but you gave me this tattoo anyway?" I asked accusingly, gripping my scratched up tattoo.

"You were better off with that black crow on your arm than this Jackson guy in your head." He squeezed his forehead and the creases were deep. "If your mom told you early on that Jackson was your dad, and he wanted nothing to do with you, you would've considered yourself a nothing—and probably would've taken that road in life that nothings go down. But instead you grew up believing your dad was something special and came from great blood. And you took the path of greatness."

"But wait," I said. "I thought you told me that I needed to get out of the fantasy land my mom created for me."

"As you were getting older, I wanted you to get things straight in your head. That's why I said that. But as a kid, you don't always need the burden of the truth, especially when the truth ain't pretty. Sometimes..." he lifted his arms and slowly twisted them as he looked at his tattoos. Then he lifted his legs, one at a time. The snake, the eagle, the lizard, the women, the cross. A smile grew, and the wrinkles around his eyes deepened. "Sometimes when the truth is that ugly," his voice went soft, like he was telling me a secret, "a story could end up being the most beautiful thing you got."

I listened to his words, really listened, and understood what he meant. It was kind of the same thing my mom was trying to say that day in the turquoise room. My mom couldn't change the facts of my life, so she changed the story of my life and gave me something better to believe in. And, it turned out to be my own truth in the end. Faris was probably right—she did okay with me. I lifted my eyes toward the sky, squinting at the brilliant afternoon sun. I was thinking that maybe one day, after my mom and I finally talked everything out, I could tell her that she did okay.

There was someone else who did okay with me. And he was right there by my side—just like he'd been since I was twelve. "It always helped having you around, Faris," I said. "I'm not sure I would've turned out okay without you being here for me."

He squinted his eyes and nodded. His wrinkles were as deep as ever, and looking at all that ink on his head, I was reminded of how scary he looked to me when I first met him. I could have never imagined back then how important Faris would become for me—a father figure and a friend. He was someone to count on, someone who loved me when he didn't even have to.

I didn't take him as the kind of guy who would want sentimental talk, but I felt like I needed to say more to him. Just a little more to let him know how much he meant to me. I looked down at my hands, hoping I could say what I wanted to say without my voice cracking. I felt tears coming, but I managed to hold them back. "Maybe," I said, my voice a little shaky, so I straightened up and cleared my throat. "Maybe it was really you and your friendship that's the most beautiful thing I got."

He didn't say anything right away, just kept looking out at the traffic. I wondered if he thought I was being too sappy. I tried thinking of something else to say to get things cool between us, but I was at a loss.

And then I saw him wipe his eye on his sleeve. "Thanks, kid," he said quietly. "That means a lot."

I leaned back against the brick wall. I could tell he got what I was trying to say. Without any more words between us, Faris lit one more smoke as he and I went on to share yet another Hollywood afternoon together. It was a pretty quiet and uneventful afternoon, but for some reason, it felt like one of the better ones.

Acknowledgments

Special thanks to the Edith Kanaka'ole Foundation for allowing me to use Edith Kanaka'ole's beautiful chant "E ho mai" in the novel. My fellow writers and dear friends, Eric Rankin, Robert Woodcox, and Pete Kalionzes, thank you for all of your writing support over the years. Thanks to Kenny Picquelle for being my "tattoo advisor." Lily Richards and Casperian Books, thank you for believing in my novel. And thank you to my husband, Tony Sary, for always supporting my dream.

25518

CPSIA information can be obtained at www.ICGtesting.com
Printed in the USA
BVOW04s1219230614

357083BV00001B/7/P